SOPHIE'S TREASON

SOPHIE'S TREASON

Beverley Boissery

A BOARDWALK BOOK
A MEMBER OF THE DUNDURN GROUP
TORONTO

Editor: Barry Jowett
Design: Alison Carr
Proofreader: Allison Hirst
Printer: Webcom

Library and Archives Canada Cataloguing in Publication

Boissery, Beverley, 1939-
        Sophie's treason / Beverley Boissery.

ISBN 10: 1-55002-642-9
ISBN 13: 978-1-55002-642-9

        1. Canada--History--Rebellion, 1837-1838--Juvenile fiction.
I. Title.

PS8603.O368S643 2006   jC813'.6   C2006-904261-6

1   2   3   4   5   10   09   08   07   06

 Conseil des Arts   Canada Council
du Canada   for the Arts   Canadä
                                        ONTARIO ARTS COUNCIL
                                        CONSEIL DES ARTS DE L'ONTARIO

We acknowledge the support of the **Canada Council for the Arts** and the **Ontario Arts Council** for our publishing program. We also acknowledge the financial support of the **Government of Canada** through the **Book Publishing Industry Development Program** and **The Association for the Export of Canadian Books**, and the **Government of Ontario** through the **Ontario Book Publishers Tax Credit program** and the **Ontario Media Development Corporation**.

Care has been taken to trace the ownership of copyright material used in this book. The author and the publisher welcome any information enabling them to rectify any references or credits in subsequent editions.

J. Kirk Howard, President

Printed and bound in Canada
Printed on recycled paper

www.dundurn.com

Dundurn Press
3 Church Street, Suite 500
Toronto, Ontario, Canada
M5E 1M2

Gazelle Book Services Limited
White Cross Mills
High Town, Lancaster, England
LA1 4XS

Dundurn Press
2250 Military Road
Tonawanda, NY
U.S.A. 14150

For Susan Pieters
with love and gratitude.
Thanks a lot, Susie Q!

They called him The Loon.

He knew that wasn't his name. He knew what loons were, remembered watching a pair of them one summer on a lake. Where the lake was, though, he didn't know. But he did remember being awed by their ability to dive straight into it from the air, and that someone had told him they could dive at least one hundred feet. And he remembered feeling melancholic as he listened to their plaintive cries at sunset.

It was strange. In his mind's eye he could see the two loons swimming. He could even recall grinning as he watched their mating dance. But when he tried to think where it had happened, the familiar blackness was like an ocean of darkness in which his mind's pictures of the loons shone like a sunlit globe. He felt like a disembodied eye that had this one vision. For a while, he wondered if this was how God saw the universe, and if the earth was like that globe.

Of course, he knew he wasn't God. Maybe he was in hell, although he'd always thought it must be bright from all the fires, not like this constant darkness. For all he knew, he could be dead and six feet underground.

Then, he heard soft voices. The women were back. They spoke French as they whispered to each other. A strange kind of French, but French nevertheless. That made no sense either. As he lay quietly, trying to find something to help him understand, he heard someone else enter the space. He recognized the sound of boots on bare floors. The stranger muttered something in English and immediately pain stabbed the Loon's head, like a pin being jabbed into a pincushion.

He fought the pain, trying to stay awake to learn something from this Englishman he somehow associated with brutality. He listened while the man questioned the women brusquely, and smiled as they answered more and more slowly while the Englishman sounded ever more impatient. He felt he could see the man's hand and see a finger punching the air as he spoke, because the jabbing pain in his head became more and more intense.

Someday, he thought, he'd understand. Someday, he'd answer the Englishman's questions, and someday, he promised himself, he'd thank the women for their protection.

CHAPTER ONE

In December 1838, Montreal was a sullen city. Most residents scurried about their business with grim efficiency. The *joie de vivre* for which the city was famous seemed a thing of the distant past. Every jail was full to overflowing. People looked at each other carefully, worrying that strangers might be informants. Smiles seemed yet another casualty of the recent rebellion.

Sophie Mallory was as sullen as the city as she traipsed along Notre-Dame Street with her friend Luc. Sullen, and scared. She couldn't begin to imagine what trouble she'd be in if her guardian, Lady Theodosia Thornleigh — her father's fiancée and one of the richest women in England — ever found out. Lady Theo had told her several times that morning that she was not to leave the house. And she had emphasized that Sophie was not to go with Luc.

But, what choice did she have? Two months earlier, she hadn't known Luc existed. In the short time she'd known him, he'd become her best friend. She could not possibly have let him face this morning's ordeal alone.

She'd met him and his brother Marc at her home in Malloryville, Vermont. For a while, he had been a mystery. She'd see him only in the distance. When her brothers' children tried to beat her up, Luc stormed to her defence. Her next meeting with him was equally dramatic. She'd come to Lower Canada to visit Edward and Jane Ellice, Lady Theo's friends from London. They'd had no premonition that a rebellion would break out, much less that they would become the rebels' prisoners. When Sophie became separated from Lady Theo, Luc rescued her and just before the rebellion ended, he risked capture by coming to tell them the unbelievable news that her papa had been taken prisoner as well. Surprisingly, the British army had captured him, and that made no sense. Her papa was no rebel.

To help prove this, Lady Theo leased a house in the Montreal suburb of St. Lawrence and, in Sophie's opinion, began spending almost all her time in lawyers' offices. Sophie quite liked the house. Not as much as she liked her home in Malloryville, of course, or even the London mansion she'd lived in until six months ago. That had been really grand.

This Montreal house was relatively new. Ivy had only tangled its branches halfway up the grey stone walls. The house was big, with eight bedrooms. Sophie had chosen one that looked out across snow-covered fields to Mount Royal, the mountain after which Montreal was named. The view helped her feel less homesick. Some mornings, while waiting for hot water to be brought up to her, she lay in bed imagining that she was back in Vermont and looking out on her beloved Mount Donne.

There was one huge disadvantage to the house, which Sophie realized only gradually. It was isolated, a long twenty-minute walk from the city. She was so grateful that Lady Theo had invited Luc, who was an orphan, to live with them. Without his company, she would not have known what to do with herself. She sometimes wondered if that was the main reason that Lady Theo had taken him under her wing and protected him against arrest for his own part in the rebellion.

She hated that word: rebellion. Sometimes she wondered if even the idea of it turned men mad. It had been a disease in her own family since the infamous Boston Tea Party of 1770, and it seemed to be in Luc's as well. That was why she was bundled up and unhappily trudging along a muddy street so early in the morning. At ten o'clock, Marc Moriset, Luc's brother, would be one of the first rebels to stand trial for treason. If the mood of passersby was any indication, he'd probably be sentenced to death by hanging.

When they reached the courthouse door, Luc used his shoulders to push through the crowd of people and soldiers, pulling Sophie inside with him. Only when they were in the back entrance of the courtroom did he stop. It was packed to the rafters.

Sophie took quick, hurried glances around the room. "There," she whispered finally. "On your right, near the wall towards the front. By the fat man in the blue jacket. I think there's just enough room for us."

"For two sheets of paper, maybe," Luc muttered.

Sophie re-examined the room, looking for an alternative. It was built like a theatre, with the seats at the back higher than those in front. Braziers provided warmth for those fortunate enough to sit close to them. The front row of seats was empty, but roped off. She looked at Luc in exasperation and pointed to the small space again. "Can you see anywhere else?"

Luc also looked around the room before shaking his head. "Come on then," he muttered eventually, taking her elbow and leading her down towards the front of the room. "You'd better do the talking."

Sophie understood. It was the French-English thing. Luc obviously thought the fat man was English. The relatively small English minority in the city had been outraged by the rebellion. If the fat man was English and typical, he'd want to vent his displeasure on the closest French-speaking person, and that would be Luc.

Some spectators in the courtroom huddled together in groups, for warmth as well as protection. Most wore distinctive homespun cloaks with colourful sashes around the waist, indicating that they were farmers from the countryside surrounding the city. For a moment, Sophie thought about suggesting that she and Luc try to cram themselves in with them, because she felt a sudden sense of kinship. Like them, she was an alien.

Instead, she walked down the aisle towards the front as grandly as she could, reminding herself that she was not only Miss Sophie Mallory of Malloryville, Vermont, but also Miss Sophie Mallory, ward of Lady Theodosia Thornleigh.

"You go first," she told Luc, once they reached the front. She let go of his arm and followed as he carefully stepped over people's feet, finding his way to the space near the wall. Squirming and wriggling into it, they sat in silence, ignoring the muttered complaints of the man sitting next to them.

Eventually Sophie turned to look at their neighbour. His ears were huge and his ruddy cheeks bulged as he methodically chewed something. Probably tobacco, she thought, after catching a glimpse of his brown teeth. His clothes looked as though they might have been fashionable five years earlier but smelt like they hadn't been washed since the summer. There was an expression on his face that Sophie couldn't figure out. In her experience, fat people were happy. She remembered the cook in her father's London house. Not only had she always had a supply of treats ready for Sophie, but she'd made her feel welcome.

This man seemed a different story. When he turned his head and caught her studying him, Sophie blushed and stared at her feet instead. She hadn't quite envisioned this discomfort when she'd agreed to accompany Luc. For several self-pitying moments, she wished she had sheltered behind Lady Theo's orders and refused to come to the courthouse. Then the man stood up, almost squashing her toes when he stepped on them.

Oblivious, he faced the back of the room, calling out to some friends sitting in the back rows. "Glad to see you lot got in. Hope it's worth the effort."

"Of course it will be," one of the men shouted back.

"What do you think, Alf? Think the judge will sort this lot out?" another asked.

"Shouldn't need a judge," Alf, the fat man, grumbled loudly. He waved his hand in emphasis, almost knocking Sophie's bonnet off her head. Ignoring her cry of protest, he raised his voice, "Should have saved ourselves a lot of money. Should have strung the whole lot of them up on the lampposts. Every man jack of 'em. A reb on every post. That would make 'em think about rebelling again."

"Wouldn't be able to think then, Alf," one of his friends told him. "They'd be...." He broke off and made screeching noises as he tried to imitate the sound of someone suffocating.

Alf roared with laughter, only to stop in surprise when an elderly gentleman tapped him on the shoulder from behind. "Listen, Alf," the stranger told him. "The young lady next to you is an old friend. Now, my seat's back with your friends. I think we should change, don't you? It would make sense. You'll be able to chat more easily and I think you'll have more room."

Sophie watched in astonishment as Alf allowed himself to be gently pushed towards his raucous friends, slightly awed by the elderly stranger's air of authority. She turned as Luc nudged her and whispered, "Do you know him?"

Sophie shook her head slightly. "Don't think I've ever seen him."

"What do you think he wants?"

It was a good question. After their new neighbour settled himself, he pulled a slim writing tablet and a silver propelling pencil from the inside pocket of a grey frock coat and seemed content to sit quietly. Luc nudged

Sophie again, and again Sophie shook her head, positive that she'd never met him. Finally, when her curiosity seemed about to burst, the stranger turned and smiled.

"Miss Mallory? It is Miss Sophie Mallory, isn't it?"

Sophie scented danger and glanced at Luc. He, too, looked wary, poised to run, if he had to. Stilling him with her hand, Sophie turned back to the stranger and inclined her head graciously as she'd seen Lady Theo do more times than she could remember. An "I know you are in the same room as I am, but I do not know if you deserve to be" kind of look.

Instead of being intimidated, the stranger smiled reassuringly. "No, you don't know me. Nor should you. But a few weeks ago I admired your throwing accuracy in a certain incident outside my hotel, then I found out who you were. I'm Robert Christie from the city of Quebec. Retired barrister. At your service."

Sophie blushed. That "certain incident" Mr. Christie mentioned was something she had hoped no one would remember. Her much older brothers — Albert (known as Bert), Bartholomew (or Bart), and Clarence (whom everyone called Clart) — had sent Mrs. Bates, their housekeeper, into Montreal with two thugs to kidnap her and take her back to Vermont. She'd managed to escape by making balls from the fresh and slightly frozen manure on the street. While Luc held off the thugs with well-aimed snowballs, she threw her manure-balls at the housekeeper. She'd known the fight had attracted a crowd, and had prayed she'd never meet anyone from it. She glanced at Luc, but he simply grinned and looked away.

"Of course, you had help then," Mr. Christie smiled as he continued. "A peasant woman. The same height as your young friend, I believe."

That also was true. Luc, wanted by the British for his part in the rebellion and in danger of being recognized, had dressed up as a woman to try to find her. That Mr. Christie should have put two and two together was unnerving, and Sophie saw from Luc's compressed lips that he was suddenly scared, and maybe wondering if the friendly retired lawyer could be a government spy.

They took safety in silence, once again staring at the floor. In the background, Alf and his friends competed for the honour of being the most obnoxious people in Montreal, or perhaps on God's Earth. They shouted out to all and sundry their particular brand of political wisdom — how they'd govern the province if they had a chance, and what they'd do with its French residents. Hanging seemed to be their consensus.

When a door at the front opened, even they became silent.

CHAPTER TWO

Like everyone else, Sophie watched as a man entered and began scurrying around, straightening chairs. After a few seconds, she frowned and grabbed Luc's arm. "Something's wrong," she told him. "We're in the wrong room."

Luc looked at her. "Are you serious? We can't be. Look how crowded it is."

Sophie tried to imagine what other trial would draw so many spectators, then stubbornly shook her head. "I don't know," she finally said. "But, Luc, look at the front."

In front of them a scarlet-draped table dominated the room. It was massive — maybe as long as forty feet — and at least three feet higher than anything else. There were fifteen chairs set at regular intervals behind it, two desks at each side, and a long enclosure with a roughly built bench on the right, between it and the spectators. Several furled Union Jacks stood in their standards behind the table, adding vivid splashes of red, white, and blue to the sombre room and giving authority to the table.

As Sophie and Luc watched, the clerk self-importantly tidied the fifteen stacks of paper and the inkwells that stood in front of each chair. "What's the matter, Sophie," Luc whispered, studying the table again. "What's worrying you?"

"Well, I can't see where the judges are going to sit," she whispered back. "Can you?"

The government had gone to a lot of trouble to make the room look as majestic as possible, presumably to symbolize its authority. Surely, the powerful judges should have had the place of honour. But, try as she might, Sophie couldn't see where they'd sit, unless it was in the roped-off section right in front of them. That couldn't be right, she knew, because then they'd be among the spectators.

Mr. Christie cleared his throat and tapped her on the arm. "I really do beg your pardon, Miss Mallory, but I couldn't help overhearing. I can answer your question, if you'd allow me to."

Sophie smiled her agreement, then exchanged wary looks with Luc. She certainly wasn't comfortable with the way Mr. Christie seemed to know everything, and she could see that Luc was still on edge, as though wondering why the lawyer had chosen to sit with them. Maybe he thought Mr. Christie planned to point him out to the police constables in the doorways. As Lady Theo kept reminding them, these were desperate times and desperate people were doing anything they could think of to gain the government's favour.

Mr. Christie seemed not to notice their cautious reactions. "The reason you're not seeing a place for judges, Miss Mallory, is because this isn't an ordinary trial. It's a court martial. Do you know what that means?"

"A court martial's a trial for soldiers in the army," Luc answered.

"Right ..."

"But my brother isn't in the army. So, how can they try him here?" Luc blurted out, and then went deathly white as Sophie gasped. If Mr. Christie was a government spy, Luc had just about handed himself over for arrest. Desperate people, desperate times, she thought as she looked at Mr. Christie in panic.

He seemed to be mulling something over in his mind. The list of defendants, it turned out. He held his hand out to Luc. "Mr. Moriset, I presume."

Luc looked stricken, torn between good manners and petrified about the consequences of being identified. For the first time, Sophie understood exactly why Lady Theo had warned them time and time again to be careful. By letting his guard down for that tiny moment, Luc had given his identity away to a total stranger. She wondered how much Mr. Christie knew about the rebellion and if he realized that Luc was still wanted in the area south of the St. Lawrence.

Mr. Christie withdrew his hand without making an issue of it. "Maybe you would be well-advised to wear women's clothes again tomorrow, Mr. Moriset. Like you did when you helped Miss Mallory in her, er, snowball fight," he said quietly. "There are many spies in the room and once the novelty wears off, they'll be studying everyone even more carefully. Today, though, you can be part of my family."

Luc looked like he wanted to cry, and Sophie knew how annoyed he was with himself. In an attempt to distract him, she turned to Mr. Christie. "I don't know anything about court martials," she admitted. "Could you explain it to us, sir?"

"Courts martial, Miss Mallory. One trial is a court martial; two or more, courts martial. I suspect there will be at least ten trials before we're done," he stated, and Sophie decided that he really must be a lawyer. Or a grammar teacher. No one else would care whether it was court martials or courts martial. But when he went on, she could tell he was really talking to Luc, not her.

"A lot of lawyers do not understand it either. Personally, I don't think it's even legal for the government to try civilians here. But, with the army everywhere, who can say it's wrong? Not me, that's for sure. I'm not that brave. In any case, that's why twelve very ordinary men will be tried for treason this morning with the soldiers they fought against as their judges. There'll be General Clitherow...." He broke off and looked directly at Luc. "Do you know who he is?"

Luc nodded. "He's smart. He commanded the troops at Napierville, and he's Governor Colborne's right-hand man."

"That's right. He'll sit in the middle in the big chair, as he's in charge. He'll have four colonels, three majors, and seven captains as his fellow judges. The desks on the left side are for the deputy judge advocates. They're lawyers — barristers like me, really. As deputy judge advocates, though, they tell the officers what the law is and act as the prosecutors."

Sophie felt outraged by the thought of officers who had fought in the rebellion judging its participants. "That's not fair. I saw what the Glengarries did in Beauharnois when they rescued us. They didn't care about the law or if people had rebelled or not. They just burnt their houses down anyway."

"It really doesn't seem right, sir," Luc added so quietly and nervously that Sophie could see he still didn't trust Mr. Christie at all. "Some of the men's farms are threatened by English settlers. How can British officers understand that?"

"They can't," Mr. Christie retorted. "They know how to fight, how to advance against the enemy in straight lines, when to charge, when to retreat. Most importantly, they know how to follow orders. They understand discipline, young man, not the law. They won't care if someone is a soldier or a farmer. All they know is that these men rebelled against the British Crown. According to the law, that is treason. Everyone seems to have decided already that they're guilty, and the government has said they must be punished. You'd better prepare yourself, young Luc. There'll be no compassion here today, I'm sorry to say."

Sophie knew that Mr. Christie was being kind and, as he said, preparing Luc for the inevitable. Still, the worry she'd managed to keep at the back of her mind suddenly leaped to the front. Was this the kind of justice her papa would have to face?

No one seemed to know why he had been arrested. Benjamin Mallory had crossed into Canada to attend a Welcome to Winter party at the Beauharnois country house of Lady Theo's friends from London: Edward and Jane Ellice. When Benjamin hadn't arrived in Beauharnois, Sophie and Lady Theo assumed he had waited for the rebellion to end before travelling north to Canada. They hadn't known Benjamin had left

Vermont until Luc found out that he was in a jail somewhere south of the river. Lady Theo vowed to get him
out of prison, but Sophie wondered if she really could.
Would Papa end up having to face trial in this room, in
front of those fifteen officers — the general, the four
colonels, the three majors, and the seven captains?
Beside her Luc was obviously fighting his own demons
of fear. "I've heard my brother has a great defence," he
whispered to Mr. Christie, blinking hard. "That has to
count for something."

"I...." Mr. Christie stopped when he heard a slight
commotion behind them.

"Oh, no," Luc said, elbowing Sophie in the ribs.
"Don't look up. She's here."

His suggestion was too late. Sophie had already
turned to see what was happening. A small group of
fashionably dressed people was walking down the steps
to the front of the room. Among them was a tall
woman dressed entirely in black, from her sable cloak
and muff to her highly polished boots. A few tendrils of
blond hair escaping from her black fur cap gave her a
deceptively ethereal look.

Lady Theo!

Sophie found she could hardly breathe as she looked
straight into her guardian's stern eyes. Eyes that promised retribution for Sophie's disobedience in leaving the
house. Before anything could be said, Lady Theo's

escort tugged her arm and they seated themselves inside the roped-off enclosure, just as the nearby door opened and the first prisoner was led into the courtroom.

Immediately, Alf and his friends shouted insults at him. He kept his composure. Not looking to the right or the left, he walked to the bench on the right, the chains on his hands and feet clanking dully. As Alf's friends shouted their predictions about the fate he could expect, another prisoner followed, then another. Several must have had a rough time as they were brought through the crowd outside the courthouse, and Sophie cynically wondered how carefully their soldier-guards had protected them. Traces of yellow splattered more than one coat, obvious remnants of rotten eggs that had been hurled at them. A few men touched welts on their faces where stones must have hit them. All rubbed their hands and she saw red rings where handcuffs had bitten into their wrists.

Caught up in noticing these details, she missed the twelfth man at first. Then she saw his face and heard Luc's gasp. Marc Moriset was well-dressed, his dark frock coat contrasting with the short jackets worn by the farmers among the accused. Tall and proudly defiant, he looked back into the room at Alf and his mates and, not surprisingly, his look of disdain acted as a red flag to their blood lust. Their feet drummed on the floor as they shouted insults and punched the air with their fists.

"Hey, look at him. Look at that stiff-necked Frenchie," Alf shouted.

"Just think of this, boys," one of his friends responded. "Hey, Frenchie. By the end of the week, that neck you're so proud of will be stretched another twelve inches by the hangman's rope. What will you think of that, Jean-Claude or Pierre or whoever you are?"

Alf's friends laughed and some made creaking sounds, noises presumably meant to sound like Marc's neck as it took the weight of his body on the gallows. Sophie wished she were still a child and could cover her ears. Then she heard Luc sob. When his hand slipped into hers, she knew she had been right to disobey Lady Theo and come to court with him, no matter what punishment she'd be given. They sat hand in hand in silence, while it seemed half the room shouted insults and invectives. Sophie wanted to throw up at the thought of her father sitting on that roughly hewn bench, and she realized anew how hard it must be for Luc now that he saw what little chance Marc had.

"Tell him not to listen to them. Tell him to block his ears," Mr. Christie said quietly.

Sophie squeezed Luc's hand more tightly. "Don't listen to them, Luc," she repeated. "You have to believe he won't die. In any case, don't hide. Look at him. Let him see your face. Let him know that someone in this horrible crowd cares about him."

Immediately, Luc straightened his back and looked at the prisoners. As Sophie watched, he managed to catch his brother's eye, and lifted his hand. For a few seconds, Sophie thought that Marc wouldn't respond, but then he suddenly grinned. Immediately, Alf's friends began another round of outrage and the sergeant-at-arms had to pound on the floor for silence. When they quietened reluctantly, the sergeant ordered everyone to stand. The officer-judges marched into the room and stood behind their chairs.

They looked impressive in their full dress uniforms with every brass button polished to a shine. Gold epaulets gleamed. Most wore scarlet coats, others the blue or green of their various regiments. Every man wore a fierce, proud expression. They were so immaculate that, at first glance, they could have been mistaken for a box of toy soldiers come to life. Only when Sophie looked closely did she see they looked as tough as nails. Mr. Christie had indeed been right when he'd warned Luc not to expect compassion from these fifteen men.

Sophie didn't understand much of what happened next. While she had been looking at the officers, two civilians had entered the courtroom and seated themselves at the desk near the prisoners. She assumed they were their lawyers. One stood and spoke to the judges for what seemed an interminable time. Sophie knew whatever he said was serious, for Mr. Christie made notes and Luc listened intently, but she could make no sense of it. Judging by the commotion Alf and his friends were making behind her, they didn't either.

"What's going on?" she finally asked.

Mr. Christie held a warning finger up, scribbled a few more words, then whispered, "They're telling the judges that this court is illegal and ..." he held his finger up again, seeing Sophie about to ask another question. "What they're really saying is that the British army cannot take over from the courts here. That the prisoners should be tried in a regular court, according to regular law, and not by this court martial and military law."

"Are the two laws different?"

"Very much so," Mr. Christie answered grimly. "You'll see."

What Sophie saw for the next few hours was a lot of boring talk. At first, it was funny in a sad sort of way. The word the prisoners' lawyers used for "illegal" was "incompetent" and, naturally enough, the very competent soldiers couldn't believe their ears.

"He's saying that I'm incompetent?" Sophie heard one of the majors fume.

"Not just you, Jack," his neighbour answered. "He's saying the whole ruddy lot of us are as well. Now keep quiet."

The major subsided in silence but he looked unhappy and, as Sophie watched, he wrote furiously on the paper in front of him. But this was the only excitement, and soon Sophie lapsed back into her thoughts. She had no idea how Lady Theo would punish her disobedience. She didn't care really, as long as Lady Theo didn't wash her hands of her and send her back to her brothers in Vermont.

She wished they knew exactly where her papa was and why the government seemed determined to keep his whereabouts a secret. Surely, someone should have realized that if Papa was in England when the rebellion was being planned, he could not have been one of its masterminds. How could he have met with the rebels in Montreal? He hadn't left Malloryville until he'd come north to attend the Ellices' party and been captured. And surely Edward Ellice's father, "Bear" Ellice, one of the richest men in the entire world, would not have had Papa as a friend if he'd been plotting against his government. That had to count for something.

But being in the courtroom had given Sophie an idea: what if she and Lady Theo went to a proper judge, not one of these officer ones, and swore on the Bible that Papa had lived in London and had only come back to Vermont in September?

Luc appeared lost in his thoughts as well. He didn't seem as bored as Sophie felt, but he looked as though he were someplace else. Someplace sad. Trying to imagine where that might be, Sophie was surprised when everyone stood suddenly and the officer-judges filed solemnly out of the room. A babble of noise broke out, people stretched, and Mr. Christie turned to them. "Well, that's it for today. The court's adjourned till tomorrow. I'd be honoured if the two of you would be my guests for luncheon. You must be hungry by now."

Sophie hadn't realized she was hungry. Nor had she thought about eating. She looked at Luc, raising her eyebrow in an unspoken question. Before Luc could answer, Lady Theo walked across to them. "Children," she said. "Now, please."

Sophie smiled her thanks at Mr. Christie as he stood to let her pass, and Luc thanked him for his invitation and shook his hand. Then they meekly followed Lady Theo from the room, using the door at the front rather than the one at the back that everyone else had to use. Bailiffs and constables scurried to open doors for Lady Theo as she swept past them and into the frigid outdoors.

John Coachman had the carriage waiting. "Home, John," she said to him, and once they were on their way, she looked sternly at Sophie. "We will not discuss this morning until luncheon is finished. Then I want a full explanation."

CHAPTER THREE

It was a sombre meal and, as soon as they had finished, Lady Theo suggested they retire to the back parlour.

Sophie felt as though the sword of Damocles hung over her when she entered the room. Lady Theo arranged the chairs so that she and Luc sat close to the fire. Close to its warmth, but to its light as well. Sophie thought she'd done it deliberately and felt aggrieved. While Lady Theo's face would be hidden by shadows, her own would be as transparent as daylight.

For a few long minutes the three of them sat in silence. Luc fiddled with things on the table beside him and Sophie fervently wished she was anyplace else. Lady Theo seemed content to let them fret. Just as the silence became unbearable, she cleared her throat and turned to Sophie. "Now then, young lady, what was the last thing I said to you this morning?"

"That you supposed you had no control over what Luc did but that *I* had to stay in the house all day," she answered sulkily.

"And did you?"

Sophie glared. "You know I didn't."

"Yes, I know you didn't. What I don't know is why you would disobey me."

"Someone had to be with Luc."

"And I planned to be," Lady Theo answered sharply. Then she sighed and leaned forward, letting Sophie see the lines of exhaustion and worry on her face. "Sophie, child, this is a horrible situation for all of us. Unless we trust each other, it can only get worse. Can you understand that?"

After Sophie nodded her head, she went on, "What have I told you ever since we came to Montreal?"

Sophie quickly looked across to Luc. This wasn't the scolding she'd expected. "That I had to watch what I said because we could all get into trouble. That if I said the wrong thing and the wrong people heard me, we could all be charged with treason."

"And, today you saw just how serious treason is, Sophie. That could have been any of us on trial. A couple of the things we did during the rebellion made us just as guilty as some of those men."

Luc nodded, his face haggard. "I feel terrible, Lady Theo. I know that I'm far more guilty than some of them. More than poor Lesiège, for sure. He's just there because they've mixed him up with someone else. But when General Clitherow made his speech, telling us that treason was the worst of all crimes, I thought he was looking straight at me."

"It's not fair, Lady Theo," Sophie burst out. "Mr. Christie, the man who explained everything to us, thinks the judges have already made up their minds. They're not going to listen to anything — they're going to find everyone guilty."

"They shouldn't be judging them anyway," Luc added. "Like Sophie said, they fought against them. They can't possibly be neutral. Maybe we need another rebellion to make sure they treat us fairly."

"That's enough, Luc," Lady Theo said sternly. "That's just the kind of talk the government wants to stop. As much as I hate to say it, I think your Mr. Christie was right. The verdict has already been decided. I'm sorry, Luc. Desperately sorry for Marc and the other men. I'm afraid, however, that you have to prepare yourself to accept the worst."

When Luc choked on a sound that was suspiciously like a sob and buried his face in his hands, Sophie dragged her chair closer to him, then turned back to face Lady Theo. "You shouldn't have reminded him."

Lady Theo ignored her and spoke again to Luc. "I'm only trying to help you understand. I looked at those officers' faces carefully today. They mean business, I'm afraid. However, that's not why I wanted to talk to both of you."

She waited until she had their complete attention. "Sophie, I gave you a direct order this morning when I told you to stay here. Now, why do you think I'd do that?"

Sophie squirmed in her chair, her fingers twitching on the armrests. She couldn't gauge Lady Theo's mood and didn't know whether she should brazen it out or be contrite. "Maybe because you didn't want me to get hurt in the crowds?" she responded, half-flippantly. "Or maybe you didn't want me to see the courtroom because I might worry too much about what would happen to Marc and Papa?"

"I had both those reasons in the back of my mind. Neither was the main one. Now tell me, either of you: you saw the people in the courtroom today. What did you notice about them?"

Luc looked across the room to Lady Theo, his attention diverted from his brother's fate. "A lot of ugly English who wanted my brother's neck stretched by the hangman's rope."

"Well, yes. They were unforgettable," Lady Theo replied. "But think. What other groups were there?"

"I suppose there were other English, the ones like Mr. Christie," Luc said grudgingly.

"And the country people," Sophie added, thinking back to the jammed stairwells and the smell of food in the courtroom. A few had looked resentful and seemed willing — like Luc — to start another fight. Most had seemed fearful, as though they, like Lady Theo, thought the verdicts were a foregone conclusion.

"Think. Harder," Lady Theo responded. "There was one more group."

Sophie shut her eyes. She visualized Alf's friends behind her and the country people sitting silently on the left side of the room. "I know. Priests. There was a group of priests!"

Lady Theo smiled. A tired smile that really didn't erase the sadness and exhaustion on her face. "And did you look at any of their faces, child?"

Sophie turned to Luc. He shrugged. "I saw Father Labelle of Châteauguay on the stairs, and I did wonder if Father Quintal had come across from Beauharnois."

"Then you didn't recognize anyone else? Either of you?"

Again Sophie and Luc looked at each other and, again, Luc shrugged. They shook their heads as they turned to face Lady Theo again.

She pursed her lips. "Yesterday, Sophie," she said quietly, "I found out that your brother, Bart, is in Montreal."

Bart was the most anti-British of Sophie's brothers. He was also the father of the boy Sophie loathed most in the entire world: the sneaky, manipulative Elias, whose main delight appeared to lie in tormenting her. She would be defenceless against him if she had to go back to Malloryville without her father or Lady Theo or Luc to help her.

"Are you sure?" she asked, feeling her heart drop to her boots. "I didn't think he would allow himself to even touch British soil."

"He came here to the house and talked with John Coachman, pretending he was lost. John recognized him, but didn't let on. He says Bart's hurt and can only walk with a cane. That's probably why I recognized him today. I can't tell you if he's come to find out about your papa, to see what's happening with the trial, or, Sophie, to try to take you back to Malloryville. I wish I knew, but I don't."

Sophie clutched Lady Theo's hand, words gushing as she fought her fear. "You won't let him, will you? I promise I'll never disobey again. I'm sorry for today. Truly. I won't ever disobey you again."

"Ah, Sophie. Of course, you will. Disobey me, that is." Lady Theo laughed a little and tried to smile reassuringly. "You've such a big heart, child. But things are so complicated. If your brother wants to take you back to Vermont, I could fight him. In court, of course. But, legally, I have no right to keep you with me."

Sophie saw that Luc looked as astonished as she felt. "Why not?" she asked. "You're Luc's guardian. I thought you were mine as well."

"I'm Luc's guardian because Marc and his grandmother want it. They are even making it legal because she's far too sick to look after him. As well, if Marc is found guilty, he forfeits everything, including his right to look after Luc. So, you see, dear child, I've more right to have Luc here with me than you. I have his grandmother's permission, and if Marc is found guilty and the courts formally approve our petition, I'll have legal custody."

Sophie had known a little of this but, until that morning, hadn't been terribly interested in the legal niceties. Now she understood what an incredibly generous thing Lady Theo had done. If things went badly for Marc, and with Luc's grand-mère so close to death, Lady Theo would look after him.

"But, what about me?" she asked. "Papa told me that I should think of you as my new mama and do what you tell me to do when he sent us off to Beauharnois. I know he gave you that piece of paper to show the guards at the border when we left Vermont. I saw it. It said you had his permission to bring me here."

Lady Theo sighed. "*Had*, Sophie. That's the problem. I *had* it ... but I don't have it now. I don't know where it is. I didn't have it on me when we were captured.

I was in my nightclothes, remember? I did send someone, a couple of weeks ago, to search the manor house for it, but they couldn't find anything. I sent another messenger down to New York hoping that he could catch up with Edward and Jane. It was too late. They had already left for England. I've written to Edward in London, but it will be months before I get an answer. Even then it may well be that Edward is tired of being involved in our affairs and won't help."

Sophie was startled to see tears in Lady Theo's eyes. Both she and Luc waited motionless while she dabbed them away, "At the very least, I'm hoping he will send back an official affidavit confirming that your papa gave me temporary custody of you. Of course, all this becomes irrelevant once we find Benjamin. I'm sure we'll have him out of prison before we can hear anything from London. In the meantime, if your brother wanted to take you now, I don't know how I could stop him."

"Papa put me in your care and if a judge doesn't understand that, he's stupid," Sophie muttered resentfully. She stared at the intricate red and gold pattern of the Bokkara rug on the floor in front of the fire, then stood and faced Lady Theo. "I will not go back to Malloryville without you or Papa. I don't care what any judge says. I won't go back. If Bart tries to kidnap me, I'll scream and say he was a rebel or something. I'll tell on him. He's the one who got Papa into trouble."

Both Luc and Lady Theo looked at her. "What do you mean?" Luc asked.

Sophie shrugged. "It's the only thing that makes sense. He and Clart are always doing things that don't work. When I was little, Papa was always getting them out of trouble. I bet they're involved in this."

"Marc is something like that," Luc put in. "Sometimes he doesn't know when to stop. He keeps going and going until he's gone too far. Not always," he qualified. "Just sometimes."

Sophie opened her mouth to say something, but Lady Theo held up her hand. "Tell me later. I still have to meet the lawyer this afternoon. However, in the meantime, I want you both to be very careful if you see a limping man around. Sophie, I meant what I said earlier about trust. We have to trust each other. Maybe I should have told you why I didn't want you leaving the house today, but I didn't want to add to your worries. Now you know."

"I'm sorry," Sophie said as she kissed Lady Theo's cheek. "I should have realized you had a good reason. But I thought no one would be with Luc, so I had to go."

"I'll do my best to be with him tomorrow, but I also have to deal with the lawyers. Things were difficult already without the complication of Bart."

"I don't need anybody to go with me to court," Luc muttered. "I'm not a baby."

"No, you're not," Lady Theo answered. "In fact, if you will agree to two conditions, I'll entrust Sophie to you tomorrow."

Luc immediately straightened his shoulders and Sophie could see that Lady Theo had managed to give him back his pride. His voice sounded confident as he said, "I'll do whatever you ask, my lady."

"Well, three things, actually. From what I've been able to discover, the Montreal police aren't looking for you. They have their hands full with the seven hundred men already in jail. As long as you're careful and don't look for trouble, I don't think trouble will find you. But you must keep a better guard on your tongue, Luc. You need to appear uninvolved, particularly if I'm to vouch for you. The lawyer and I are working on getting permission for you to visit the jail after the trial to see your brother. So, watch yourself in the courtroom, please."

"Agreed," Luc answered in a voice that cracked, and Sophie guessed he realised that Lady Theo was again gently warning him that Marc would probably be hanged.

"Second," she went on in a much brisker voice. "You must allow John Coachman to go with you and you must stay with him the entire time. I need to have your word that you won't try to run away from him."

"Agreed," Luc said again. "And the third thing?"

"You must protect Sophie. I'm worried about Bart coming here to the house. John Coachman thought he was spying out the lay of the land, so to speak. So, Luc, do I have your promise?"

Luc looked outraged. "You had no need to make that a condition, Lady Theo. It's like you said earlier. About trust. You should know by now that I'll do whatever it takes to protect Sophie. Always."

"I can protect myself," Sophie interjected.

Both Luc and Lady Theo ignored her and just nodded at each other. As Lady Theo turned to leave the room, Luc gave her a quick hug. "Thank you for your care of us," he said. "I know neither of us deserves it, but thank you anyway."

Sophie kissed Lady Theo goodbye. Luc gave her a quick peck on the cheek as well, then grinned. "There's one more thing," he said. "Something to keep our spirits up. Marc's got a crackerjack defence. I listened carefully to what they charged him with, and I think he'll get off, because he didn't do what they said he did."

The Loon felt stronger the next time the Englishman with the boots came to see him.

His head no longer ached as badly, and he had become accustomed to the constant darkness. He knew by now there were bandages over his eyes, and although they were changed daily, it was only done at nighttime.

He wondered why the nuns were so careful about this. Four of them were responsible for his care. Sisters Marie-Josephte and Celeste during the day; Jeanne-Thèrese and Ursuline at night. He had learned a lot about them.

Sister Celeste, who didn't speak English, was the most gentle. When she changed the bandages, she didn't pull the scabs off. She soothed his face and gently massaged the pins and needles out of his legs. She, more than any of the others, always untied his arms while she worked.

Judging by the clicking of beads, Sister Ursuline was the most devout. Sometimes he lay awake, terrified, and only the soft sound of her rosary reassured him that someday things would be right in his world. Without ever saying a word, she was the one who gave him the most hope.

Sister Mary-Josephte was the most curious. She wanted to know all about him. His name, where he had come from, how he had become so badly injured. He got tired of saying, "I don't know," to everything. Sometimes he answered, "Je ne sais pas." The fact that he knew a little French puzzled both of them.

He often wondered if she believed him, if she had any idea of the enormity of what he didn't know. He thought she was beginning to understand that he was speaking the truth and that he really could not answer her questions. She was always present when the Englishman came but he thought she stayed for his protection rather than to satisfy her curiosity. "Finis!" she'd say and the Englishman accepted her authority and walked away.

One afternoon he caught Sister Marie-Josephte by surprise. "Ask me about loons, if you want me to tell you something," he told her.

"About loons? The birds?"

"Oui, soeur. I can tell you about their beauty, about the moment they enter the water from the air, about sitting by a lake at dusk and listening to their cries. About how they mate."

She let him talk, both of them amazed at the torrent of words that poured out. When they ebbed, she asked softly, "And, monsieur, where is this lake?"

The Loon was silent for several long minutes. "Ah, soeur," he said finally. "May your good Lord help me. I don't know."

She stood up, suddenly all briskness. "Well, tomorrow we'll know more. We'll take the bandages off just before noon. We'll give you a mirror, Monsieur La Lune. And then, you'll see."

As she bustled from the room, he crashed back against his pillows, utterly defeated. If two faces appeared in the mirror, he knew he wouldn't be able to tell which belonged to him. He had no idea what colour his hair was, or his eyes. He didn't know if his nose was straight or crooked, if his Adam's apple jutted out like the highest peak in a mountain range or if he had a dimple in his chin. All he knew was when he looked in that mirror tomorrow, he'd see a stranger.

However, he'd found something out to add to his meagre collection of facts. For the first time the implication of his name had registered. He'd somehow always heard "Loon" when the sisters talked to him. Sister Marie-Josephte, though, had clearly said, "Monsieur La Lune."

He wondered why they had called him that. Because he was crazy, a lunatic? Or, maybe, because he had come to them on a moonlit night? Tomorrow, he thought. Tomorrow, he'd ask.

CHAPTER FOUR

Luc's optimism was contagious. For the first time in a couple of weeks, Sophie didn't cry herself to sleep. The next morning Lady Theo was as good as her word. She assigned not only John Coachman to go to court with Luc and Sophie, but Thomas, one of the new footmen she'd hired, as well.

"I'll come as soon as I can," she assured them before leaving for the city herself. "I'm hoping for some definite news at long last about your papa, Sophie. Then, I have a meeting with your trustees, Luc. Don't worry about luncheon. I've told the men they are to escort you to Orr's." She smiled a little at Sophie's reaction to the name of the hotel. "Don't pout, child," she went on. "No one will remember you from that incident."

Luc shook his head vigorously. "Begging your pardon, my lady. You're wrong. People wouldn't forget anyone who threw manure at people in a Montreal street. They certainly haven't forgotten a pretty girl doing it. Particularly in front of the second best hotel in the city."

Sophie blushed and slid a little lower in her chair. "I don't want to go there. Not so soon. Can't we go to Rasco's?" She had nothing but fond memories of Montreal's best hotel.

"Orr's is closer to the courthouse," Lady Theo answered. "Just hold your head high, Sophie, and don't show your embarrassment. I've reserved a private parlour. It's the best I can do."

Sophie pouted for another moment, then realised that her problems were minor compared with those of Luc and Lady Theo. She smiled in apology. Before she could say anything, Luc got up and walked around the table to Lady Theo. "Thank you for what you're doing for us, my lady," he said gruffly. "Lunch in a private parlour, even one in Orr's, will be more than welcome." Then, to Sophie's great astonishment, he raised Lady Theo's hand and kissed it in a very formal, very French way.

"Oh, be off with you," Lady Theo said, albeit with a smile. "You'd better hurry if you want to get a seat. And remember, keep your mouths shut. Both of you. You saw what people were like yesterday. If they even suspect someone's a rebel, they won't care whether they're guilty or innocent. You don't want to draw attention to yourself. Not with what you know."

When they entered the courtroom about half an hour later, Sophie found it less intimidating. For one thing, Mr. Christie had managed to save a couple of places for them, and for another, she realized that she could ignore Alf and his friends at the back of the room. Luc's obvious confidence in his brother's defence gave her a sense of hope.

Her optimism faltered a little after the officer-judges marched in and the court martial recommenced. Almost immediately she saw that several prisoners looked angry and frustrated. A couple seemed to object to what was happening, but Sophie couldn't understand what they were saying until Mr. Christie translated their objections for her. To that point all the testimony and bickering back and forth between the lawyers had been in English. She'd thought that natural. Mr. Christie, though, wondered how many of the men actually spoke or understood English. Sophie asked Luc.

"Probably only four," he answered angrily but softly. "I don't see why they can't have interpreters."

Mr. Christie shrugged. "That's only one of many things I don't understand," he answered dryly. "These men are farmers, not soldiers. If this were a criminal court, their lawyers could speak for them. Instead, as we'll see today, they have to be their own lawyers while the government uses two of the best in the entire province. It's madness," he finished, shaking his head in disgust.

Sophie immediately thought of her papa. She knew that, even as clever as he was, he'd find it difficult to act as his own lawyer in front of this court martial. She turned to Luc, wondering if he'd known exactly what handicaps Marc faced. To her amazement, he didn't look perturbed. "Don't worry, Sophie," he told her a little smugly. "Marc can take care of himself. You'll see."

Although the testimony that morning had little to do with Marc, it was still fascinating. Most of the defendants had been involved in a curious incident the Saturday night before the rebellion began. In Châteauguay, a neighbouring village of Beauharnois, the rebels had been led by Joseph-Narcisse Cardinal, a lawyer. Like Marc, Cardinal wasn't one of the top leaders, although, again like Marc, he appeared to know their plans. What he hadn't known, however, was the part he and his men should play in the rebellion.

By listening to the testimony, Sophie pieced together their story. When they met the Saturday night of 3 November, they dithered and dilly-dallied about what they'd do. Some wanted to be part of the attack on Edward and Jane Ellice's manor house in Beauharnois, others wanted to go off to join the main rebel group in Napierville. Eventually they decided to get some extra weapons from the Mohawks on the nearby reserve of Caughnawaga.

And so they set off, about eighty of them, in the dark. As they stumbled their way through the woods, they lost track of each other and were heard by a native woman searching for a lost cow. She ran back to her village and told the elders about the large number of men in the woods. About dawn the Mohawks challenged some of Cardinal's men. As the rebels prepared to fight, one of their leaders, Maurice Lepailleur, stepped forward. "Don't shoot," he told the men. "We've come to get guns, not hurt anyone."

The Mohawks quickly rounded them up and took them at gunpoint across the frigid St. Lawrence to Montreal in their canoes. Thus, these would-be rebels were in jail before the rebellion even broke out. After the Mohawks finished testifying, a local magistrate named John McDonald corroborated the story, adding his reason for the whole fiasco: rebellion against the queen.

Sophie thought that was ridiculous. How could an attempt to borrow guns be rebellion? Obviously, though, the officer-judges thought it was if the captain closest to Sophie was any indication. She'd never seen anyone sit at attention before. She hadn't thought it possible until she'd seen him. He stared at the prisoners with a supercilious look on his face and not once did she see him blink. His folded arms were held slightly in front of his medalled chest and he sat so rigidly that he might well have been a statue.

Once the prisoners began cross-examining the witnesses against them, Sophie wondered if, secretly, he might have found the goings-on as silly as she did. It was like a three-ring circus. The accused asked their questions in French. These were first translated into English for the officer-judges, then into Mohawk for the witnesses. The answers were translated into English only.

After realizing this, Sophie turned to Luc. "It doesn't seem fair. No one tells them the answers. What's more, I can't see what Marc had to do with any of it. None of them have even mentioned him."

She'd no sooner got the words out of her mouth than Magistrate McDonald was recalled to the stand for the sole purpose of implicating Marc. A tall, very thin man, he swaggered to the witness stand with mincing, self-important steps. Once there he nodded to the officer-judges as though he was trying to let them know he was on their side. Marc Moriset, he testified, had crossed the St. Lawrence in the early hours of Sunday morning, the fourth of November. Sophie smiled as she thought it must have been an incredibly busy time on the river. At first light, the Mohawks had been paddling their canoes north with guns aimed at their prisoners. It must have been quite a sight and she wondered if Marc might have seen it when he was supposedly travelling south. She stopped grinning, however, as Mr. McDonald elaborated on his previous testimony.

He'd been captured by the rebels and taken to a makeshift prison in Châteauguay early that Sunday morning. Peering through a narrow slit in a boarded-up window, he had seen Marc teach military drills to the Châteauguay men and drill them daily for the rest of the week. Finally, the magistrate went on, shuddering dramatically as he seemed to remember the horrors of Saturday, November 10, Marc took him and the other captives to the main prison in Napierville.

"We were all important men," he went on, preening a little, it seemed, for the benefit of the officer-judges. "Men like Mr. Ellice of Beauharnois, as well as myself. Yet we were herded onto a cart like cattle, gagged and handcuffed."

Sophie bit back a giggle as she wondered how anyone could handcuff cattle. Mr. McDonald, however, didn't seem to notice that he had said anything ridiculous. "I will remember that morning to my dying day." His voice wavered pitifully. Probably, Sophie thought, so that everyone could imagine how horrible an experience it had been. He paused, then pointed dramatically at Marc. "And that man, there, was in charge of the convoy. He personally walked beside the cart. Every now and then he spoke. Every time he did, it was an insult to me and my queen."

"He's lying," Sophie whispered fiercely. "He has to be."

She hadn't cared much for the man until that point. But when he'd mentioned Mr. Ellice's name, her dislike escalated into something like hatred.

After her papa became engaged to Lady Theo, she'd met a lot of people like this Mr. McDonald. They floated around the fringes of English society. Generally, they would ignore her. That is, until they found out her connection to Lady Theo and, of course, to Lady Theo's brother, the Earl of Hornsby. Suddenly, she became their new best friend. Everything she said was clever. They laughed at every joke she made, told her she looked beautiful. She'd smile and try not to let her irritation show. Lady Theo had told her that was the way a true lady behaved but, inwardly, she despised them.

She looked at Luc. Surely, she thought, he has to realize the magistrate's testimony could mean the hangman's noose for Marc. This wasn't a silly attempt to borrow guns. Mr. McDonald had told the officer-judges that Marc drilled men to fight; he acted like a rebel when he commanded the Napierville escort. Luc should have been worried out of his mind. Instead, he smiled as Mr. McDonald added details to his story.

When the magistrate finished, the prisoners began, one after another, to cross-examine him. He waited for their questions with a supercilious smile. Sophie thought it was his way of letting them know that he understood more law than they did. The magistrate also seemed to take great delight in pretending that he didn't understand French, answering some questions with a dismissive shrug, others sarcastically. He was cruel as well, Sophie thought. One man had a stutter and it took him a long time to get his question out. McDonald answered them in French. Even Sophie, with her poor knowledge of the language, realized that he mocked the man by imitating his stutter.

Finally, Marc stood. Both Luc and Sophie leaned forward on the edge of their seats. In stark contrast to the prisoner before him, he analyzed the testimony against him systematically. "Mr. McDonald, did you really see me drilling men on the village square on Sunday the fourth? Is it possible you could have been mistaken, seeing that you had only a narrow slit to look through?"

The magistrate raised an eyebrow. "I was not mistaken. I saw you drill the men, just as I've testified."

Marc tried unsuccessfully a couple of times to get him to change his story. "Tell me then," he went on, seeming to give in, "why are you so positive that I was in charge of the group that escorted you from Châteauguay to Napierville the following Saturday? How is it possible that you didn't see me between the Tuesday and the Saturday?"

Mr. McDonald smiled contemptuously. He looked first to the officer-judges and then back at Marc. "Just because I didn't see you doesn't mean that I couldn't hear you," he replied. "And, when you seemed away from the village, I assumed you were off fighting Her Majesty's forces somewhere."

Marc refused to be shaken. "Sir, was I or was I not in the village on the Thursday and Friday?"

"You were in the village for part of the time."

"How do you know that, Mr. McDonald?"

"I know it because I saw you."

"And on the Saturday, are you sure you are not mistaken? Remember, sir, you are still under oath. Are you positive that I commanded the men who took you to Napierville?"

This time the magistrate made no attempt to hide his contempt as he looked first at Marc and then at the officer-judges. "How many more times must I tell the court this? You were the man who walked beside me, taunting me the whole way."

Marc obviously sensed the officers' patience running out. "How can you be so certain it was me?" he asked hurriedly.

General Clitherow raised his gavel, but Mr. McDonald plainly was relishing his chance to be the centre of attention. "Because," he replied, grandstanding once more as he pointed at Marc. "You, sir, have a face that once seen is not easily forgotten."

Everyone laughed and Marc blushed. That last bit, about Marc's good looks, Sophie thought, was the only part of the magistrate's testimony that sounded true. Marc *was* exceptionally good-looking.

After Mr. McDonald was excused from the witness box, he strutted towards a seat in front of Sophie and Luc and sat there, smiling complacently. He had done his job. Deep in her heart, even Sophie wondered why Marc had challenged him by asking so many questions. He must have realized that the answers made his conviction more certain. Certainly, his cross-examination had not shaken the magistrate at all.

Luc's smile, though, was wider than ever. "Why are you so happy?" she whispered. "What on earth do you have to smile about?"

Before he could answer, General Clitherow adjourned the court for luncheon. Everyone stood as the officer-judges left the room. Then Mr. Christie turned towards Luc and Sophie. "May I take you to lunch today?"

Sophie frowned, not sure if Lady Theo would approve. Luc, though, had no hesitations. "Sir, we'd be honoured if you would be our guest. We have a private parlour reserved at Orr's, which is, I believe, your hotel."

During lunch, while Luc told funny stories about his school, she distracted herself by looking around the private parlour. It was almost a replica of one at Rasco's. Did every parlour in Montreal hotels look the same? she wondered. Well, not exactly the same, but they all seemed to have the same decor. At Rasco's the striped wallpaper above the wainscoting was blue, to match its prized Wedgwood Willow patterned china. Here, at Orr's, the wallpaper's stripes were a soft wine colour and cream.

When Mr. Christie laughed, Sophie switched her attention back to Luc. The morning's testimony should have scared every wit he had, she thought sourly. Instead, it appeared to have made him deliriously happy. Sophie wasn't sure how to react. She didn't understand his manic need to laugh or joke. Neither, apparently, did Mr. Christie. After the dirty plates had been cleared and tea and cakes brought in, he cleared his throat.

"You seem very cavalier about this morning's testimony, young man. I thought you might need consolation. Instead, I find myself entertained."

Luc sobered almost immediately. "I'm sorry. I feel desperately sorry for Mr. Cardinal and the others. I do. But, I'm so happy for Marc. He told a friend that he was going to set a trap and I think Mr. McDonald walked right into it. Otherwise, Marc would never have repeated the questions."

Sophie thought back to the magistrate's testimony. "I didn't see any trap," she said. "I thought Mr. McDonald was oily. I looked at the officers, though. They seemed to find him convincing."

"Convincing? You'll see."

To Sophie's surprise, Lady Theo arrived. She looked momentarily disconcerted to find Mr. Christie with them, and as Sophie introduced them she wondered if another scolding lay in store for her when they went home. After Mr. Christie resumed his conversation with Luc, Sophie whispered to Lady Theo, "I hope you don't mind — about Mr. Christie, that is. He's been kind to us."

"It's fine, child. I'm not upset with you."

But you are upset, Sophie thought. "Did you find out anything new about Papa?"

She bit her lips when she realized that her whispered question had captured Mr. Christie's attention, and turned to Lady Theo with an apprehensive shrug. "Mr. Christie's a lawyer. Maybe he can help us."

Lady Theo's mouth thinned into a polite smile. "I doubt it."

Mr. Christie looked embarrassed. "I'm not aware of your problem, my lady. If it has a legal nature or is something to do with the current political state, I'd like to offer my services. I'm in a unique position, you see. Beholden to no one. I've retired from my practice in the city of Quebec. Furthermore, I have no aspirations to be a judge or to go further in my profession. This means I'm answerable to no one, my lady."

He broke off for a moment and seemed to consider what he was going to say carefully. "If your problem concerns the events of the past month, I understand that legal representation might be difficult to obtain, things being the way they are. No one wants to go against the government. At the moment, its powers seem limitless. Two judges have already been punished for deciding a case according to the law instead of the governor's command. And, of course, there's the future. Governments seem to have long memories and can affect a man's livelihood as well as his career."

As he shrugged, Sophie wondered what he meant. Her papa had always grumbled about governments' short memories, but Lady Theo nodded in agreement.

That small nod of her head seemed to encourage Mr. Christie, for he continued. "What I meant, my lady, is that the government cannot intimidate me. I have nothing to lose. So if I could be of service, I'd be delighted to help."

Lady Theo looked at him carefully, and Sophie could see her thinking something over. After a few seconds she smiled. "Well, sir, if you can explain why habeas corpus doesn't work in this city, I'd be grateful."

At the question, Mr. Christie's face lit up. "My lady, the whole issue of habeas corpus has become very murky indeed this past year."

"So I've gathered," Lady Theo said dryly.

Sophie and Luc stared at each other in total incomprehension. "What's habeas whatever?" Luc asked.

Mr. Christie cleared his throat. It was Lady Theo, though, who after a quick look at her watch, rushed to answer. "What it means in England, Luc, is that if someone is arrested, his family has to be told what prison he is in or where he is."

"You mean...." Sophie suddenly understood why Lady Theo looked so angry and frustrated. She must have been trying to get the lawyers to use this habeas thing to find out where her papa was, and they couldn't do it. But before she could finish her question, Lady Theo rose from the table.

"It's time we headed back to the courtroom," she announced, putting a hand on Luc's shoulder. "Are you prepared for this?"

"I can't wait, my lady. I'm positive that Marc will get off."

When he nonchalantly flicked a speck of dust from his jacket, Sophie felt afraid. She could easily see that he believed the afternoon court session would be just as trivial as that speck. As he led the way back to the courthouse, he swaggered, and Sophie became even more frightened for him and his brother.

The Loon stared into the mirror Sister Marie-Josephte handed him.

He had black hair. Well, mainly black. The hair near his temples was white and that surprised him. He hadn't imagined himself old enough to have white hair. Almost every inch of his face was covered in bruises: fading yellowy, greenish ones to be sure, but evidence that he had either been in a horrific accident or been beaten within an inch of his life. The most sinister piece of evidence for this was a deep cut running from his hairline, through his swollen right eye, to his cheekbone.

He now understood why he had been kept in a darkened room and why his head had been almost continually swathed in bandages. He remembered old Jackman getting a cut like the one he had and losing the sight in his eye when he'd walked into a stack of swinging lumber. Suddenly, that scene was vivid: the rope on the block and tackle that was beginning to fray, the tremendous amount of blood, and the horrible sadness he'd experienced later when he'd explained the accident to Jackman's wife.

For a moment, he felt elated by this memory, but when he tried to extend that scene there was only the familiar blankness. He had no idea where it had taken place, except it had been in a wood mill. It irked him that he should remember Jackman's face and name so clearly because he still had no idea of his own identity.

He turned to Sister Mary-Josephte and shook his head bitterly. "The face in the mirror, ma soeur, is a stranger. I'm still Monsieur La Lune, I'm afraid. Do you know what happened to me? How I got these wounds?"

She looked at the door. "The English, monsieur," she whispered in a tight voice. "They brought you here half-dead. It is indeed only because of the good Lord and our prayers that you live."

"You're forgetting the care you took of me."

"Non, non, monsieur. We have looked after many people. But only one or two worse than you. Believe me, it was the good Lord." She stopped as they heard a commotion in the distance. "Quickly," she whispered. "Back into bed. We will say nothing yet of this. He must not know that you can see."

The Loon allowed his face to be re-bandaged and his good arm re-tied to the bed frame. He lay as still as he could and was not surprised when he recognized the sound of boots on the floor. He thought he'd never forget their noise as long as he lived. He listened to the rapid questions and again took delight in Sister Mary-Josephte's slow replies. Her patient was progressing but very slowly, she told the Englishman. Did he want to see for himself?

"Yes."

The Loon could feel Sister Mary-Josephte's distress as she slowly took the bandages off his face. He made certain to keep his eyes closed, as though he were still unconscious. The Englishman stood and seemed to look at him for an extraordinarily long time before he turned away and started towards the door. As soon as he heard the footsteps, the Loon took a quick look at him.

The Englishman was dressed in the scarlet uniform of a British officer. The Loon had a blinding impression of golden epaulets on the soldier's shoulders. The boots were the kind of black that meant champagne had been mixed with the boot polish to give that particular sheen, though how the Loon knew that he didn't know.

Lastly, he looked at the man's profile.

To his surprise, he felt a visceral emotion, something like a mule's kick to his gut. He might have expected himself to feel fear, given his situation. Instead, he knew he despised this British officer with his glossy boots. Why that should be so was just another puzzle for his tired brain. One puzzle too many for that particular day.

CHAPTER FIVE

After they returned to the courtroom and settled back into their seats, Sophie worried more than ever that Luc's certainty about his brother was nothing more than a pipe dream. Just before the proceedings resumed she asked him, "Are you sure Marc has an ace up his sleeve? These officers mean serious business, Luc. They wouldn't even let Lesiège go. Everyone knows he's innocent. Even their own witnesses."

A little of Luc's cockiness left him and he seemed, for that moment at least, to contemplate the possibility of his brother being found guilty. "That was bad," he admitted slowly. "I don't understand why they can't free Mr. Lesiège. Why make him stay chained up?"

"If they released him, he could act as a witness for the defence, my boy," Mr. Christie said, shifting his attention back from habeas corpus. "They must not want him testifying. I can't think of any other reason."

As Luc snorted his disgust, the fifteen officer-judges marched back in and the proceedings resumed with several of the farmers making pathetic attempts to defend themselves. "Oh dear," Mr. Christie commented softly after one particularly inept bit of cross-examination. "That poor man just proved the government's case against himself."

Finally, it was Marc's turn. He stood, tall and confident, as he recalled the first witness against him. That man had testified that Marc arrived in Châteauguay late on the Saturday night, November third, the very night Sophie and Lady Theo had been captured just a few miles away in Beauharnois. That seemed so long ago, an almost forgotten time. Sophie had trouble matching her experience with the picture being painted in the courtroom.

Facing this witness, Marc asked if he remembered the weather that Saturday night.

The man scratched his head. "Not particularly."

"Would you say that it was stormy?"

"It might have been."

"In fact, it was stormy. Do you remember that?"

"It might have been," the witness repeated. It seemed his set answer to everything.

"Well then," Marc went on relentlessly, "do you

remember that the ferry from Montreal could not cross the river because of that storm?"

The witness hesitated for several long seconds. "I remember the ferry being shut down one night about then," he answered eventually.

Marc dismissed him and called the Montreal harbour master. Luc's smile became broader as his brother systematically proved that the weather had been indeed so bad that the ferry had been unable to steam across the turbulent St. Lawrence on Saturday, November 3.

A stocky man wearing well-worn leather waistcoat took the witness stand after that. His shirt was dirty and rumpled and his boots looked like they had never seen the contents of a tin of boot polish "What is your occupation?" Marc asked.

"I work in Pierre Tremblay's stable. At the hotel near the wharf in Lachine."

"And did you see me the morning of Sunday, the fourth of November?"

"I did. You came several times to see if the ferry was able to cross the river."

"When was the latest time you remember seeing me?"

"Lunch time. I remember giving you a slice of pork because you were so hungry."

"Could I have been in Châteauguay before two o'clock that day?" Marc asked.

most damning witness of all against him. Magistrate John McDonald swaggered to the witness stand just as he had before. He stood, facing Marc, a picture of confidence.

Again, Marc was systematic in his cross-examination. He took the magistrate through his testimony, re-establishing in everyone's memory exactly what the magistrate had said against him. He concentrated on two points: that Mr. McDonald had seen him drilling the rebels on the Sunday morning and that he had commanded the rebel escort detail that transported McDonald and the other prisoners to Napierville the following Saturday. The magistrate did not alter his testimony. He had seen Marc Moriset in command on both occasions.

Marc's final question to him seemed a last-ditch effort. "Sir. Is it possible you saw someone else on those occasions?"

Before replying, the magistrate turned towards the officer-judges. Sophie imagined he might have made some kind of facial gesture showing his contempt for the question. There was no doubt of his scorn, though, when he faced Marc. "As I said before, Mr. Moriset, yours is not a face one easily forgets."

Alf and his friends sniggered in the back of the room until General Clitherow pounded his gavel on the table and demanded silence. Marc dismissed Mr. McDonald, who walked to a chair just in front of Sophie, and called a Mr. Pierre-Jacques Beaudry to the stand.

"Now, this is interesting. Very interesting," Mr. Christie murmured. Sophie saw that several other people looked puzzled as well.

Mr. Beaudry was the polar opposite of the stable hand Marc had called upon earlier. He was tall, and walked to the stand as though he were used to a parade ground. His grey frock coat was beautifully tailored and fitted him like a glove. His pantaloons were the latest fashion. A diamond twinkled from a tie-pin in his cravat. Ordinarily Sophie might have expected to have seen him at one of Lady Theo's at-homes. What such a man would be doing in a courtroom as a defence witness, she couldn't imagine.

Marc began quickly, "Mr. Beaudry, would you tell the court your occupation?"

"Certainly. I am the keeper of the Montreal jail."

Like many others in the room, Sophie gaped in astonishment.

"Mr. Beaudry, as keeper of the jail, you are responsible for knowing who is in the jail, when each man entered, and where he is kept. Is that correct?"

"Yes."

When Luc's hand suddenly squeezed Sophie's, she knew the next question was vitally important. She leaned forward to make sure she heard it.

"Then, sir, could you tell the court where I was on Thursday, the eighth of November last?"

"You were in my jail, Mr. Moriset."

"What?" one of Alf's friends shouted from the back of the room. "In jail? Before the end of the rebellion?"

"Bloody hell! The magistrate's lying," another bellowed.

In the hubbub, General Clitherow banged his gavel ineffectively. Only after he threatened to evict everyone from the room did people gradually stop talking. Luc nudged Sophie's arm and pointed to Mr. McDonald. Sophie, of course, couldn't see his face—but judging from the back of his neck, it must have been beet-red.

Once order had been restored, Marc resumed his questioning.

"Mr. Beaudry, you know how crucial this testimony is. Could you tell the court if there is any possibility that I could have taken Mr. Ellice, Mr. McDonald, and the others from Châteauguay to Napierville on the morning of Saturday, November 10? One witness has sworn several times upon his oath that I did so."

Mr. Beaudry beckoned to somebody standing in the doorway, who struggled forward and handed over a bulky book. Then he faced the officer-judges. "This, gentlemen, is my prison register. You may examine it if you wish. It will show that once Mr. Moriset entered my jail on the eighth, he remained there until yesterday morning, when he was brought here for trial. He could not have taken anyone to Napierville on the tenth of November. He was a prisoner in my jail."

"You see," Luc told Sophie excitedly, "I told you old McDonald was lying."

General Clitherow beckoned to the deputy judge advocates and announced a short recess. As soon as the officer-judges left, people began talking excitedly. Some seemed, like Luc, elated. Others, puzzled. Alf and his friends sounded as though this was the best entertainment they'd been to in years.

The officer-judges filed back in after about fifteen minutes. Court resumed when General Clitherow pounded his gavel and demanded order. After the spectators quietened, he recalled Mr. McDonald to the witness stand.

McDonald was a different person when he walked forward. Vastly different. Gone was the magistrate's swagger, his air of importance. He was perspiring heavily, Sophie saw, and when he reached the witness stand he made no attempt to stand straight but instead slouched against the wall at the back as if he needed its support. Once again he was asked if any of the men in the courtroom had taken him from Châteauguay to the rebel prison in Napierville.

"No," he said quietly and without the air of vindictiveness that had marked his earlier testimony.

"Speak louder, man. Remember you are still under oath," General Clitherow cautioned in a way that let everyone know his disgust. "You must have more than that to say."

"No, sir," McDonald repeated in a voice that was only a trifle louder. He looked at the general, saw the unyielding expression on his face and sighed. "I must have been mistaken. You have to see it's understandable. We were so tired and terrified about what might happen to us."

"Understandable?" someone called out in derision. "And Moriset with that unforgettable face?"

"Damned coward," one of the officers muttered as his hand crushed a sheet of paper into a ball.

"Your witness," General Clitherow said to Marc.

Sophie thought it was to his credit that Marc didn't let any expression show as he began another cross-examination. "Mr. McDonald, previously you told the court that once seen, mine wasn't a face a man could forget. Now, it would seem, I must have a very ordinary face. One so ordinary that you could mistake it for whomever your captor was on the road to Napierville."

"Ask a question or dismiss the witness," General Clitherow interjected.

Sophie wished she knew what he was thinking. He sounded angry, but she didn't know who he was angry at. Mr. McDonald, for sure. But Marc as well, if the way he glared at him was any indication.

Marc faced him. "Sir, I don't think I will get an answer to the questions I want to ask. I want to know why this man, a previously respected magistrate, would stoop to lying to convict me. I had thought being captured was the worst thing that could befall me. Now, I see it is the hand of providence. Would anyone have believed me otherwise when I said I had no part in taking the prisoners to Napierville? Would you have believed that a gentleman of Mr. McDonald's reputation, a man sworn to uphold the law, would bear false witness against me? Tell me, what does it bode for any man who cannot produce an unimpeachable witness to undo the lies? Can any prisoner expect justice from this court, I wonder?"

"Oh, dear," Mr. Christie said softly. "He's gone too far."

Sophie looked at General Clitherow. Although he said nothing, but simply waved Marc back to the prisoners' bench, she saw that his lips had thinned and that his eyes flashed fire. Just moments before she had tried to find any expression on his face. Now that Marc had attacked him and his court it was obvious. He looked grimly resolute, like a man who knew only one way to respond to attacks. He would fight back.

"The court will adjourn for an hour and a half," he announced. "At that time we will hear the prisoners' closing remarks." With that he rose and, followed by the rest of the officers, left the room again.

Mr. Christie stood and offered his arm to Lady Theo. "Would you care for a cup of tea, my lady? As you know, it's a short step to Orr's."

"Will we miss anything?" Luc demanded.

Mr. Christie smiled. "No, young'un, you won't."

Nevertheless, as they waited in a parlour in Orr's for afternoon tea to be served, Sophie felt anxious. When she looked at Luc, he seemed nervous as well, now that Marc had made his feelings about the court-martial much too clear. No one had any appetite.

"What do you think will happen?" Sophie asked Mr. Christie while one of the maids poured tea.

Mr. Christie quickly looked at Lady Theo and Sophie saw her nod almost imperceptibly. "To be honest," he began, "I have no idea. The only person whose fate I think I have any idea about is the poor Lesiège. His only crime seems to be that he has the same name as a rebel. I think it would go against the officers' sense of honour to convict him but, I have to admit, I am not even positive about that."

"Honour?" Luc scoffed. "You heard old wind-bag McDonald. What honour is there when a magistrate lies?"

"Young man, there's a great deal of honour in that courtroom. Those officers have had it drummed into them ever since they joined the army. It's not the same as you have and maybe it's not the same as mine. Underneath everything, though, you'll find there's a sense of it. Don't forget, those men swore allegiance to our young Queen Victoria. When they fought at Napierville, they fought for a queen whom some of them know and for whom they'd willingly give their lives.

"That's why the wording of the charge against the prisoners is so dangerous, young Luc. Your brother and his friends are charged with waging war against Queen Victoria. Here, in Montreal, the Queen is somebody in England that we don't really think about as a real person. For those officers, well, for a few of them at least, it means the beautiful young lady they have met in London and maybe danced with. To them, she's a real lady that they are ready to protect and die for."

"I've met her," Sophie interjected. "She was nice."

Both Mr. Christie and Luc ignored her. "My brother has honour too," Luc said finally. "He's fighting for what he believes in."

"There's the problem," Lady Theo commented. "Different senses of honour. In my opinion, the tragedy is what happens to innocent people when those different senses collide."

"Like Mr. Lesiège," Sophie commented.

"Actually, Sophie, I was thinking of your father."

And with that, the all-too-familiar terror returned. Her hand tightened on the delicate handle of the porcelain cup she was holding. A slight tremor made gentle waves. She knew her papa was innocent. But could he prove it if worst came to worst and he had to face the

British officers who would judge him? The same ones Marc faced?

Her stomach churned as they walked back to the courtroom. The proceedings resumed with Mr. Cardinal, as the prisoners' spokesman, making a final plea for them. Once again, he challenged the court's set-up, asking how ordinary people could be tried under military law if they weren't soldiers.

Sophie could see that argument irritated the officers. A couple of them muttered to each other, but most simply stared at Cardinal with cold eyes. He tried a couple of other arguments. How could he and the other Châteauguay men be charged with treason, he asked, when the rebellion hadn't begun? And, he asked, exactly what had they done that was treasonable? They had simply visited their friends the Mohawks to see if they would lend some guns. Since no one fired a shot, what was their supposed rebellion? When had asking neighbours for the use of guns become treason?

He became even more scathing when he reviewed the evidence against Marc. The court needed two witnesses of impeccable character to prove treason. That was the law, he reminded them. There weren't two credible witnesses to Marc Moriset's alleged treason. One had admitted that he had been too drunk to be accurate; the other had been shown as a liar. Therefore, Marc's case should be thrown out.

Lastly, and desperately, he appealed to the officers' compassion. Ten of the twelve men were fathers, and he begged the court to consider the implications of a guilty verdict. Wives would become widows and dozens of children would be made fatherless.

There wasn't much chance of that argument succeeding, Sophie thought. She studied the grim faces of the officers as they gathered their papers together after General Clitherow once again adjourned the court. When it resumed the following morning, he would announce the verdicts.

CHAPTER SIX

When they arrived in the courtroom the following morning, they found that Mr. Christie had once again secured front seats for them. As soon as Luc sat down, Mr. Christie reached across and tapped his shoulder. "Good news. I've heard a rumour. Two men are going to be acquitted."

Luc's face brightened immediately. "Lesiège and Marc."

"It's only a rumour, Luc," Lady Theo cautioned. "Don't get your hopes up too high. If the mood of this room is any indication, people won't be satisfied with anything but hangings."

Alf and his friends had taken over the back of the room once more. Again, one of them made his stretching sound, then announced, "Them rebels are going to get theirs."

"I hate them," Sophie whispered to Lady Theo. "Don't they care that the men's families are sitting right in front of them?"

"Why should they? They're English, the most superior people on God's earth," Luc said bitterly.

"Enough," Lady Theo ordered as the prisoners, in the now-familiar chains and handcuffs, shuffled into the room. Louis Lesiège looked a little hopeful. Most faced their judges stoically but a couple of them seemed to have given up hope entirely and simply stared at the floor.

General Clitherow waited until there was absolute silence in the room. "After reviewing the evidence carefully," he began, "this court acquits the following of all charges against them: Louis Lesiège and Edôuard Thérien."

Luc slumped back in his chair as the guards released the two. "Thérien? What about Marc? What's the matter with them? Didn't they listen to McDonald?"

Sophie was equally baffled and more apprehensive than ever. After the commotion died down, people leaned forward to hear the remaining verdicts. Cardinal and Joseph Duquette, his student, received the death sentence, as did François-Maurice Lepailleur and a wealthy farmer named Jean-Louis Thibert. The remaining six prisoners, including Marc, were sentenced to transportation.

"Transportation? What on earth does that mean?" Sophie asked Mr. Christie.

"Jail, someplace other than here," he answered quickly. "Probably in one of the Australian colonies. Now, be quiet so that I can hear General Clitherow explain the decisions."

It seemed that people's respect for a man counted as much to the officers as what he had actually done in the rebellion. In their minds, lawyers and anyone associated with the law should not have broken it by rebelling. Therefore, Cardinal, his student Duquette, and Lepailleur, a bailiff, were doomed even though they had not fired a shot nor shed a drop of blood. Thibert was a trustee of his church.

That type of thinking probably explained why Marc had not been freed. The Morisets were a respected family. Luc's grandfather had been one of the first men elected to the legislature. As Marc belonged to the elite, he should not have been associated with people rebelling against his own social class. General Clitherow emphasised that particular point in his concluding comments.

Alf and his friends gave three hip-hip-hurrays and then jostled each other in their rush to the nearest tavern where they could talk over the morning's events and the upcoming hangings. People towards the front of the room exited more quietly but also excitedly. In what Sophie had thought of as the "French" section, families sobbed while their priests tried to console them.

Luc sat in stunned silence. When Sophie tugged on his arm, he shook her off angrily. "That's it?" he kept saying. "My brother's going to jail someplace I've never heard of because he's a Moriset? If that's a crime, I should turn myself in as well."

"Later, Luc. We'll talk about it at home."

"Home? Where's my home? I won't have one if they send Marc away."

"Luc, you're insulting me. Of course you have a home. With me," Lady Theo said. "Make your bow to Mr. Christie and let's go."

Luc glowered before turning to Mr. Christie and jerking his head. When Lady Theo raised her hand in a gesture of apology. Mr. Christie smiled ruefully.

"I understand, Lady Thornleigh," he said, staring at Luc with troubled eyes. "Luc has vacillated between extremes. He was certain that Marc had the perfect defence but, on the other hand, all of us tried to help him prepare himself for a verdict of death. No one thought of transportation. He certainly didn't, and he doesn't know how to react." He turned to Sophie and Lady Theo and bowed in farewell, a courtly gesture that seemed out of place in the commotion around them. "It's been my pleasure, ladies, to make your acquaintance."

"And ours, yours," Lady Theo returned graciously. "You must come to the house before you return to your home. Maybe Sunday after church? My chef may not be quite as sophisticated as Orr's but she makes a superb roast beef."

Mr. Christie smiled with pleasure. "Thank you. After church then. This Sunday." As he took Lady Theo's arm to escort her to her carriage, one of the constables ran to him and tugged on his sleeve.

"I've just heard, sir," he exclaimed. "They got the verdicts wrong. They're going to have to do it all over again."

"What did you say?" Mr. Christie and Lady Theo asked in unison.

"One of the clerks heard the deputy judge advocates talking," the constable explained as everyone in the vicinity stopped to listen. "The court martial can't sentence anyone to transportation. Particularly civilians."

Luc, who had almost reached the carriage, turned back as he noticed the pandemonium breaking out. "What's he talking about, Mr. Christie? What does it mean?"

Mr. Christie looked first at Lady Theo and then at Luc. "It means you have to be brave, young man. I think when the court reconvenes, as it looks like it must, it will sentence your brother and all the other men to hang."

CHAPTER SEVEN

"Is life really like this?" Sophie asked Lady Theo once they'd returned to the house.

"What do you mean, dear?"

"Well, like when you think the worst that could happen has happened, something even worse seems to occur."

Lady Theo nodded in agreement. "I feel sorry for Luc and partly to blame. We didn't prepare him properly."

"How could we?"

"Indeed. That Mr. Christie of yours is a wise man, Sophie. I think he was right. Luc was thrown off-kilter by the transportation verdict. Although he hated it, he must have felt relieved because it meant that his brother would not be hanged. Then, it seems, the court got it wrong."

"Just as Mr. Cardinal was telling them all along," Luc said bitterly from the doorway. "They should have listened to him."

Sophie could see Lady Theo's relief when the dinner gong sounded. "Come along," she told Luc briskly. "You haven't eaten all day and you certainly can't help your brother by starving."

"I don't feel hungry," Luc protested.

"Then you can sit and watch us eat, young man. You will need all your strength to face what's ahead and I simply will not allow you to mope about. That's the last thing Marc would want."

Those words turned out to be magic. Luc took a couple of mouthfuls of the savoury stew the cook had prepared and evidently discovered that he was hungry after all. Sophie was the one who found she couldn't eat, and she rearranged her food several times on her plate. She had no idea how they would bear Marc's hanging. When she thought about the life being squeezed out of the vibrant man she'd known so briefly, she felt sick. She didn't think she could ever go through another day like the present one had been. Yet, obviously, the future was only going to get worse.

Caught up in her gloomy thoughts, she was totally unprepared when Wynsham, the butler, entered. "A Mr. Bartholomew Mallory has arrived, my lady," he said. "I've put him in the Yellow Salon and given him a glass of sherry. He insists on seeing you and Miss Sophie at your pleasure."

Sophie's fork clattered to the floor as she pushed her plate away. "Make him go away," she implored Lady Theo.

Luc pushed his chair back and came to stand behind Sophie. He glared at Lady Theo. "Tell him that he's not welcome. He's only come to make trouble."

"Sit down, Luc. Listen to me, both of you. It's a wise man who knows his enemies. Do you know what that means?"

"That we should find out why he came?" Sophie ventured.

"Exactly. We'll finish our meal, then see him. Wynsham, you may serve dessert now," Lady Theo replied.

"I want to be there with you, Lady Theo," Luc announced.

"That's fine. The three of us will beard the monster together. Right, Sophie?"

Sophie nodded in reply. She partially understood Lady Theo's strategy. Meeting Bart would certainly take Luc's mind off his brother's plight for at least an hour. Her stomach churned, though, at the thought of seeing Bart again, and she was glad she had only toyed with her food. If she had eaten more, she would be rushing out of the room and looking for the nearest commode.

"What do you think he wants?" she asked Lady Theo. "Promise you won't let him take me away."

"I'll do my best," Lady Theo answered.

"Well, I'll promise even if you won't, my lady," Luc asserted.

Neither answer reassured Sophie. *I was right*, she told herself. *Just when things can't possibly become worse, they do.*

In some ways, Bart was the same brother she'd seen only a couple of months earlier. He had never been an immaculate dresser. He had always had the knack of making clothes age three years just by putting them on. Even worse, he had no sense of style. Tonight, he was wearing a black evening jacket with everyday brown trousers. His cravat was a spotted nightmare. But his physical appearance had changed. His face seemed haunted, his eyes shadowed. Parts of his hair had gone grey. Obviously he had hurt his leg badly because he limped over to greet them when they walked into the room. After Lady Theo sat, he flung himself into a Sheraton chair with such gusto that Sophie thought its beautiful legs would break.

She wondered what he wanted. For a few seconds she thought he might have found out where her papa was, but the look on his face belied that. Had he come to find out if she was being well-looked-after? But that couldn't be right either, because he'd only given her a quick, almost disinterested, look.

Finally, after a silence stretching almost to infinity, Lady Theo asked, "Now that we've exchanged niceties, Bartholomew, why are you here? I would have thought you'd be safer in Vermont."

"I don't know why you would say that," he blustered. Sophie guessed that Lady Theo's directness had surprised him. For some reason he had not expected her to take the initiative.

"Because I saw you at the court martial yesterday," Lady Theo replied. "You certainly looked like a man in disguise. A person who wanted to hide in the crowd. You could have acknowledged us then and, as you didn't, I wonder why."

"All right. I was there."

"And dressed up as a priest," Luc pointed out.

"And dressed up as a priest," Bart repeated as he looked daggers at Luc. "However, Lady Thornleigh, if you'd answer a couple of my questions in turn, I'd appreciate it. Clart, my brother, is missing. We can't find any trace of him, and nobody we've talked to seems to have seen him since the Thursday of the rebellion. That was almost a month ago."

"Do you mean to say Clarence took part in the rebellion here?" Lady Theo demanded.

When Bart nodded, Sophie was surprised. She was not astounded, however, given her family's hatred of the British dating back to the 1770s. Her grandfather had been one of the founding members of Boston's Sons of Liberty. After the Boston Tea Party, when the British put a price on his head, he fled Massachusetts for the wilds of Vermont's Green Mountains. He and Sophie's papa both fought in the War of 1812. It stood to reason that if Clart found out there was a rebellion against the British in 1838, he would have been the first man to cross the border into Canada to fight in it.

She looked over to see if Luc understood this and was shocked. For once, his face was impassive. There was no look of surprise and Sophie realized, at that moment, that he had known about Clart, had known he'd been in the rebellion. She felt betrayed. For several long seconds she simply stared at Luc in disbelief. She'd thought they were friends and that they trusted each other. Why hadn't he told her?

She turned her back on him. "What do you think has happened to Clart?" she asked her brother.

"I can't find out, Sophie. I haven't been able to do much because the government here would like to lock me up. But friends have looked at dead bodies in some of the morgues and swear none were him. Lady Thornleigh's my last hope."

"In that case, Bartholomew, I'm sorry," Lady Theo answered. "I didn't know anything about Clarence until you told us. I'm puzzled about one thing, though. You've asked nothing about your father. Surely you must know that he's missing as well. Aren't you interested in him? In his whereabouts? His health? Anything?"

"Of course I am," Bart responded with one of his phoney smiles. "I simply assumed you were looking after him. After all, you're British, and it's your people who arrested him, I've heard."

Sophie jumped up from her chair, becoming very brave in defence of Lady Theo. "Why are you sneering at her? At least she's trying to find him. And she's right. What is the matter with you? Don't you care about Papa at all?"

Bart smiled again. He tried to pull Sophie into his arms, but she resisted furiously. When he spoke, his voice was soft and indulgent. "Of course I care, Sophie. I care about all my family. About Papa, about Clart. And about you as well, silly-billy. You're lost to us as much as they are, you know. That is, as long as you stay here."

Sophie pushed against him until he let her go. She dawdled her way back to her chair by the fire, thinking furiously. She didn't trust Bart's new-found worry about her welfare. "Albert knows where I am," she said, referring to their oldest brother. "He had me watched. He sent Mrs. Bates up here to kidnap me."

"Of course he didn't." Bart smiled and Sophie noticed that although his teeth flashed white, the smile didn't reach mid-cheek, much less into his eyes. "Albert merely wanted to make sure that you were well-looked-after and he asked Mrs. Bates if she would be kind enough to bring you home to us. You see? We do worry and care about you." He stopped, and when he started speaking again it was as though he had just had a brilliant idea. "Listen, Sophie. I'm going back to Malloryville in a week or so. Why don't you come home with me?"

Sophie was shocked. "And leave here without Papa? Without knowing where he is? Lady Theo and I would never do that, Bart."

"I'm not talking about Lady Thornleigh, Sophie. I mean you. It would be just us Mallorys. Our family. You can either stay with me or with Bert. You wouldn't have to be in Papa's house by yourself. You can choose where you would like to live."

"Then I choose to stay here with Lady Theo. She's going to be my new mama when Papa gets here and marries her."

As if she'd given him a declaration of war, Bart's florid face seemed to swell. He made a choking sound, and Sophie wondered if he'd swallowed his tongue. Finally he stood and stared at Sophie as she leaned for protection towards Lady Theo.

"That's *if*, Sophie," Bart told her. "If Papa ever gets out of jail and comes here to Montreal. Your precious British aren't a very forgiving lot, as your friend Luc should be able to tell you." He pulled a rumpled hand-kerchief from his pocket and dabbed a couple of flecks of spittle from his chin. Once dry again, he continued, "Understand this, young lady. We're not very forgiving either. Bert wants you back in the United States and, until your papa is released, he's the head of the family. What he says goes. So that means you're to be ready to go home when I do. In a week's time. Understand?"

To Sophie's relief, Lady Theo stood as well. "I believe you're suffering under some serious misapprehensions, Bartholomew. Sophie is under my guardianship. Your papa gave her into my care and I will not relinquish that responsibility."

"My lady, you don't have a legal leg to stand on and you know it. Just make sure Sophie's possessions are packed for travel next Wednesday."

Lady Theo's smile was as false as Bart's had been earlier. "I wouldn't dream of doing so, Bartholomew. As you've remarked, the authorities here would be very interested in your whereabouts. I would have no compunction whatsoever about asking for their help next Wednesday. A police guard in front of my house will not embarrass me. Sophie will remain in my care and I'll go to court to keep her with me if I have to."

Bart stood. He looked indecisive. He seemed to need a moment or two to recover and Sophie wondered if he had actually expected Lady Theo to hand her over.

"Maybe you're right, my lady. I certainly can't go into court to contest Sophie's custody. But don't harbour any illusions. You can expect a visit from Bert. He'll have no trouble seeing you in court and no constable will stop him from coming here."

He stared at Sophie for a few long moments without smiling. It was a complicated look because it not only made Sophie feel as though he loathed her, but it gave her the impression that he didn't think she was worth the time and effort he and Bert were expending. "Don't get too comfortable up here, missy," he told her eventually. "You'll be back in Malloryville in time for Christmas. *That* I promise."

He turned to Luc and Lady Theo and made the shortest bow Sophie had ever seen. With just a mere bob of his head, Bart showed his anger and his contempt for the manners polite society demanded. "Don't bother calling for your butler, my lady. I'll see myself out." With that, he swung out of the room. Seconds later they heard the front door slam with such force that the pictures on the walls rattled.

Sophie immediately ran to Lady Theo. "You won't let them take me, will you? Please."

Lady Theo put her hands on either side of Sophie's face, forcing her to look into her eyes. "Listen to me, Sophie. Your papa put you into my care. I'll do everything I can to make sure I keep you here."

Luc watched them. "There's one really curious thing about all this," he said eventually. "Something that doesn't make sense. Bert and Bart are doing everything they can to get Sophie back to Malloryville. Yet, we all know they don't like her. Their children hate her. Why do you think they want her back so badly, Lady Theo?"

CHAPTER EIGHT

Breaking the quiet that followed Bart's departure and Luc's question, Lady Theo suggested that everyone go to bed.

"I can't go yet, Lady Theo," Sophie objected. "There's something else I want to know." She turned to Luc accusingly. "You weren't surprised to hear that Clart fought in the rebellion. You knew that he had, didn't you?"

A curious expression swept across Luc's face, a mixture of pity and defensiveness. "Sophie, Clart wasn't the only person in your family to fight in the rebellion. I'd wager Bart himself did as well. Haven't you worked it out yet? Haven't you wondered why Marc and I were in Malloryville last October? In the weeks before the rebellion began?"

Sophie felt a chill run through her. An I-wish-I-hadn't-asked-that-question chill. Once asked, though, the question couldn't be taken back. She couldn't shelter behind ignorance anymore. "Then, tell me," she responded. "Don't make me sit here all night. I don't keep secrets from you."

"It doesn't matter anymore. Keeping everything secret, that is," Luc glowered at the fire for a moment, then turned to face Sophie and Lady Theo. "We all know Marc committed treason. The fact that he actually did so is the only thing that's keeping me sane. Of course he was guilty. But it's ironic that they haven't worked out what he did. Even you two haven't put two and two together yet."

Sophie thought she kept her temper superbly. "If we're so idiotic, tell us!"

"Marc's job was to get weapons and ammunition from the United States. That's why he was in Malloryville." Luc leaned forward in his chair as though some pressure was lifted off him. When Lady Theo gasped and speculation flared into her eyes, he nodded. "I see you get the implications, my lady."

"Implications? What implications?" asked Sophie, more loudly than she had intended. "Tell me. Whatever they are. I'm not a baby."

Instead of answering immediately, Luc glanced at Lady Theo as though he were seeking permission.

"Then," he said, "you should have realized that your

brothers partially bankrolled the rebellion. Bart and Clart bought over a million dollars' worth of weapons. They hid them for us in the mountains near Malloryville."

"Ah, so that's why you were always dashing up and down the mountains." For a brief moment, Sophie felt satisfied that at least one question was answered. One reason it had taken her so long to get to know Luc was that he had always been on horseback. Then that feeling vanished as her stomach roiled as fast and furiously as the Lachine Rapids. "Bart and Clart bought a million dollars' worth of guns? I don't believe you."

"Well, they did. And, what's more, they did it twice."

"Now *I'm* having trouble believing you, Luc," Lady Theo interjected, her face filled with amazement. "Are you expecting us to believe that Sophie's brothers paid two million dollars for weapons? For guns for Canadians to use?"

Luc seemed to take an almost sadistic glee in answering. "Only one million dollars, Lady Theo. They bought one lot of guns last February. Sophie's papa was in England and they knew he'd never find out. But there was trouble. An informer tipped off the government. Bart and Clart brought the weapons across the border. Marc and some others went down to get them. Then, just as they were going to pay the half-million-dollar price, soldiers came from everywhere. Bart and Clart went back to Vermont; everyone else ran for their lives. In the confusion, no one thought about the money. So, the government ended up with the guns and half a million dollars in bank notes."

"Incredible. What incredible bungling." Lady Theo looked as though she didn't know whether to laugh or cry.

"So, then they had to do it all over again." Luc avoided looking at either of them as he continued. "This time Marc let me come along. At first, I thought it was a great adventure and I felt sorry for my friends who had to stay in school. It was tremendous fun, at first. I imagined myself as all kinds of people. General Wolfe. General Montcalm. Julius Caesar. It was the best time I have ever had."

"And then?"

"Then, things started going wrong. Little things. You and your papa were home in the big house, Sophie. We had to be careful to stay out of your way." He smiled at her, his charm taking the sting out of the words. "It was only when everyone was so worried about Mr. Ellice visiting your papa, Sophie, that I realised there was trouble. Your brothers were almost always arguing. With each other, mostly. Sometimes with Marc."

"What about?" Sophie asked, her face alight with interest.

"The money, mainly. Your brothers wanted to be paid for the February consignment. At first, Marc refused. In the end he agreed that the *patriotes* would pay for both lots. After the rebellion, though."

Sophie could easily imagine the scene. Bert would have been in charge. Clart would have blustered and Bart would have smiled his special smile that was open to any interpretation. She could see Marc standing proud and defiant, knowing he was the only buyer for those guns and that the Mallory brothers would have to agree to his terms. They would not have been happy.

"Where was Marc going to get the money, Luc?" Lady Theo asked.

To Sophie's surprise, Luc smiled broadly. "From Mr. Ellice, my lady. And from men like him. They planned to confiscate their lands and sell them off. That's the main reason they were so worried when Mr. Ellice arrived in Malloryville."

Sophie looked at Lady Theo. "But he only came down to invite us to his party, didn't he?"

To her surprise, a curtain seemed to fall over Lady Theo's face. "No, dear. He had some business with your father." She leaned back in her chair and closed her eyes, as though in thought. When she opened them, she looked first at Luc and then back to Sophie. "Do either of you have any idea just how much money a million dollars is?" When Sophie started to answer, she held a hand up imperiously. "Let me tell you. I pay less than two hundred dollars in wages to keep this house running. That's for the entire year and for two grooms, a cook, Thomas, Minnie, and three other maids. A million dollars is an enormous amount of money. So, I have to ask. Where would Bert, Bart, and Clart get such a large sum to buy the guns in the first place?"

Sophie stared at Lady Theo in total incomprehension. She had no idea. She couldn't imagine any of her brothers spending their fortunes on such a chancy prospect as selling guns to Canadian rebels, much less Albert. He was the serious one. The most business-like. She would have thought he would have stopped them from getting so heavily involved.

When Sophie woke the next morning she felt happier than she had for weeks. Marc would be freed. He'd probably have to pay a large fine. That would be fair, she thought. After all, he *had* committed treason. He just hadn't committed the particular acts of treason he'd been charged with.

Strangely enough, the courtroom was not quite as crowded as it had been the last couple of days. Alf and his friends were noticeable by their absence and Sophie uncharitably thought they must still be celebrating the guilty verdicts someplace else. Even Mr. Christie was missing.

While they waited for the prisoners to arrive, Luc shook his head back and forth a couple of times, as though trying to decide on something. Finally, he leaned across Sophie and tapped Lady Theo on the arm. "Can I ask Marc back to your house for tonight, at least?" he asked.

Lady Theo looked surprised. "Tonight?"

"Well, I don't know where else he can go. His home's been burnt down by Loyalists. Our house would be nicer than a hotel."

"Luc, I don't think he'll be set free."

"He has to be, my lady. I've thought and thought about it. The officers said it themselves. If he'd been charged with murder, they would have let him off. If it's true that they can't send him off to Bermuda or somewhere, they'll have to free him. Won't they?"

Before she could answer, a clanking sound from the hallway announced the arrival of the remaining ten prisoners. The four under the sentence of death walked in stoically, their backs straight. The only sign of emotion came when they looked into the courtroom at the spectators and saw their loved ones. They smiled briefly and only looked away when forced to face the front by the constables.

A couple of the other men appeared apprehensive as though they feared the worst. But most seemed confident as they raised their hands to greet their friends and families. Marc, Sophie noticed, looked almost cocky, as though he knew he might soon sleep in the room next to Luc's.

The sergeant stood and pounded his staff on the floor for silence. "All rise," he commanded. The officer-judges filed in. After they'd settled themselves, one of the deputy judge advocates walked to the table and began talking in a slow, sleep-inducing voice. Sophie wished Mr. Christie was sitting with them. He could have explained everything. "What are they talking about?" she asked Lady Theo after she had fidgeted and squirmed in her seat for about an hour.

"I'm not sure. I think they're saying the court martial can't make the governor of an Australian colony accept criminals from here."

Eventually he stopped speaking and Mr. Cardinal stood up. As usual, his grey frock coat was dusty and egg-splattered and his face bruised from stones that had been flung at him. Plainly, none of that mattered to him as he reminded the officers that he had never accepted their authority over civilians, that he still thought the court martial was illegal. As usual, a couple of the officers glared, but Sophie could see that a few must have been shocked by the fact that they'd had to change the sentences. Those listened more intently to him than ever before.

Then General Clitherow reached into a box and produced a black cap. As he slowly put it on his head, Luc groaned quietly. Lady Theo quickly reached across to hold his hand and Sophie shifted closer to him as ice settled in her stomach. She knew what the back cap meant.

"As we have heard," he intoned almost apologetically, "this court erred yesterday when it pronounced the sentence of transportation upon six of you. You have all been found guilty of treason and this court hereby sentences you to death. You will be taken back to the place from whence you came and held at Her Majesty's pleasure until such time as that extreme punishment will be inflicted upon you. May the Lord have mercy upon your souls."

The people around Sophie drew in their breath in a collective gasp. They seemed stunned as they stood and the officers filed quietly out. For a while the only sounds were the sobs throughout the room. After a few minutes, one of the guards stood and jerked on the prisoners' chains, shattering the quiet. Obediently the ten men stood and readied themselves for the two-mile walk back to the prison.

Suddenly Luc jumped to his feet and shouted, "Courage, Marc."

Lady Theo tugged him down immediately. "Be quiet. Don't do anything foolish. Don't jeopardize yourself. Just be quiet."

Marc's face showed his shock, although not the misery he must have been feeling inside. He turned towards his brother, standing motionless, looking at him, until the guard pulled his chain. Only then did he and the others begin to leave the courtroom, every last one of them craning their necks as they looked back frantically, concentrating on finding their families and friends. All of them knew it might be the last time they would see some of them.

Long after the men left, Luc sat hunched in his seat staring at the door Marc had walked through. He ignored Sophie's tugs on his arms until Lady Theo shook his shoulder. "Come along, Luc. You can't do anything for Marc here. Let's plan our strategy at home."

Like a general, Lady Theo marshalled her troops and, like a general, she had a battle plan. As they ate tourtière, she expounded on it.

"We'll be fighting a war, Luc. Not a battle. You must understand that. We might even lose the first battles and there is no guarantee of a win. But all of us must fight hard for Marc's life, even if it means prison."

Luc squared his shoulders. "What can I do? I'm only fourteen."

"First thing this afternoon, you go with John Coachman to Orr's and see if you can find Mr. Christie. Ask him if he'll help you word the petitions and if he will return here with you. Once Mr. Christie has written one, Sophie, you are to copy it several times in your best handwriting. Can you do that?"

Sophie nodded eagerly, thrilled to have something definite to do. She would even have thrown manure balls in front of Orr's again, if Lady Theo thought it would help. She listened to the rest of the plan, her face alight with resolve.

"Tomorrow, Luc, we shall visit your grandmother. Once she's signed one of these petitions, Sophie and I will deliver it personally to Lady Colborne, Sir John's wife. We'll explain how ill your grandmother is and that, if anything happens to Marc, you'll be alone in the world. Lady Colborne is a good woman and might mention it to her husband."

Luc muttered a few words about Sir John Colborne. Lady Theo held up her hand in a sweeping gesture that almost knocked her teacup to the floor. "Luc, think. Don't cut off your nose to spite your face. John Colborne decides whether Marc lives or dies. You can say what you like about him after he's made that decision. But, until then, I do not want to hear one negative word out of your mouth. We need John's help. Don't jeopardize it. Understand?"

Although Luc nodded, he looked mutinous. When he tried to leave the table, Lady Theo stopped him.

"I'm not finished, young man. I want you to think hard and make a list of everyone you can think of who might have some influence with Sir John. Marc's priest, or anyone remotely important. We'll ask them either to write their own petitions or sign the one you'll take with you when you visit them."

Luc folded his white linen napkin and rolled it so that it would fit into the silver serviette holder while he thought. "One of Grand-mère's friends is a Legislative Councillor. He might do something. Marc's friends won't be able to help though. They'll be too busy saving their own necks," he finished with a pained twist to his mouth.

"Then, don't go near them. Make sure you only ask people who everyone knows are loyal. If we get enough signatures, maybe Sir John will commute Marc's sentence."

"Commute?" Sophie asked. "What does that mean?"

"Probably another harsh punishment," Lady Theo answered, rising to her feet. "A substitution for hanging. It means, dear girl, that Marc will live. Later, we can work to get him pardoned."

Both Luc and Sophie rose from their chairs as well. As Lady Theo paused in the doorway, Sophie thought again that she looked like a general. Or what she imagined a general might look like as he planned his next step on a battlefield. Instinctively, she stood at attention as Lady Theo finished her instructions.

"The key thing is to get the date of execution put

off as long as we can." Lady Theo looked at Luc, commanding his attention. "You must understand that, Luc. Sir John's a good man. A good man with a hard job. Don't forget he's governing a province that has rebelled twice in twelve months. The last thing he wants is a third rebellion. He has to punish some of the leaders of this rebellion harshly. He simply has to. The government at home in Britain will demand it. If he doesn't, the English here will take matters into their own hands. You must see that."

"After being in that courtroom, I can easily imagine what that will be like," Luc said bitterly.

"So can I. It will be like Beauharnois," Sophie added, remembering the bloodthirsty faces of the men of the Glengarry Militia as they burnt houses and barns and fired their guns at almost every shadow they saw. When she brought her thoughts back to the present, Lady Theo was still explaining Sir John Colborne to Luc.

"I think he'll look carefully at Marc's trial. Particularly, at Mr. McDonald's testimony. If I had to make a wager, I'd bet that he'll postpone making any decision about Marc for as long as he possibly can. Sooner or later people will get tired of hangings and accept different punishments."

"So, if the government really has Papa and Clart in jail, we have to pray that they get their trials months from now," Sophie put in.

Lady Theo smiled. "That's it, exactly. For Marc, for your papa, and your dratted brother. We must get the day of final reckoning, for all of them, postponed. The longer, the better."

The one marvellous thing about being desperately ill, the Loon thought, was that once he began to recover, he could see himself becoming a little better each day. He was now able to stay awake and had only occasional headaches.

Of course, neither he nor the nuns ever mentioned this to the Englishman with the boots. It seemed a game to the sisters and the Loon had no idea why it should be so. But they gave the Englishman as few details about his recovery as they possibly could until, one day, their pretence came to a crashing halt.

They'd had no warning of his presence. Nor did they know that this particular time he'd brought a fellow officer with him. One moment the Loon was playing a game with grey and white stones on a black and white checkered board. He laughed as he listened to Soeur Marie-Josephte's stories of her former life when she'd been in charge of nursing in Montreal's Hôtel Dieu. She'd been glad to retire to the countryside, she told the Loon. Very glad indeed to get away from the city's smells and noise. The Loon had been caught up in imagining her in the city, coping with its hustle and bustle. When he looked up, he saw someone he recognized.

"Charles," he called out joyfully. "What on earth are you doing here?"

There was a sudden silence. One that might have lasted till eternity, except that the Englishman broke it with a harsh laugh. "See, sir, it's just as I told you. He's been playing games with us."

"Games? What is this?" Sister Marie-Josephte said scornfully, defending the Loon as a mother would her young. "He plays the games with me, monsieur le capitaine, not you."

The Loon sat quietly, looking in confusion at the man he had called Charles. For one instant he had claimed a piece of his past, though what it meant he had no idea. Now, Charles was a stranger and a fearsome one at that. From looking at his uniform, the Loon knew he was a full-fledged colonel in the British army and someone to whom the booted Englishman deferred.

The gold on his jacket flaunted the might and power of British majesty, but something in his face suggested wisdom. A twinkle in the eyes hinted at kindness. And it was with kindness that he took the Loon's scarred face in his hands and examined the wounds gently.

"You've had a rough time of it, my friend," he said after a few minutes.

Friend, the Loon thought. He was right. Colonel Charles Whoever-he-was knew him as a friend. Suddenly he was scared and felt a desolating pain. No longer would he be able to shelter behind his memory loss. He felt naked and extremely unwilling to explore a world in which he had no identity.

"So," he said finally, breaking another long silence. "You are Charles and we know each other." When the Colonel merely smiled, the Loon gathered himself together and with all the courage he could muster continued, "Might I trouble you by asking for introductions?"

The booted Englishman made a hoot of derision, but his superior officer held his hand out first to the man on the bed. "Benjamin Mallory, I'm Charles Grey."

Charles Grey. Son of Earl Grey, a British prime minister, a member of the aristocracy.

The Loon's head ached almost as much as it had a couple of weeks earlier. He could now remember going shooting with Charles Grey. Remembered sitting across from him at a dinner table with a huge silver epergne between them and talking around it. He even remembered what they had spoken about.

But of Benjamin Mallory he still remembered nothing. He knew he wasn't English. That was somehow certain, but how would he have met a prime minister's son in London if he wasn't English? Yet, he knew with absolute certainty that he had not only met Earl Grey's son but had been friends with him.

Colonel Grey seemed comfortable with the ensuing silence. Eventually, though, he stood and laid a hand on the Loon's shoulder.

"Don't force it, Benjamin. I've some matters to look into for Sir John," he said, and, evidently seeing the Loon's lack of comprehension, he explained, "Colborne. Sir John Colborne. Acting governor of the province. Surely you remember him?"

The Loon shook his head.

"No matter. The important thing is that I can't visit you for at least two to three weeks. I have to go to Upper Canada, Benjamin. When I come back I'll bring a mutual friend. Someone I know you'll want to see." He clasped the Loon's hands in a long gesture of farewell, then spoke softly to Sister Marie-Josephte for a few minutes and left the room, followed by his subordinate.

Immediately, the sister bustled over. "It's good, n'est ce pas. You have a friend."

"And another as well. According to the Colonel, he's someone I'll want to meet," Benjamin answered quietly. "I wonder who he is."

CHAPTER NINE

Everyone worked frantically throughout the days that followed. Mr. Christie drafted petitions, subtly changing them for different recipients. Sophie dutifully copied them. Luc and Lady Theo were hardly ever in the house as they sought out every possible bit of support for Marc from friends and acquaintances.

One day, though, they arrived back together in the middle of the afternoon and called Sophie into the front parlour. Of all the formal rooms in the house, Sophie liked this the most. It hadn't been modernized, like the salon. It still had an elegant simplicity, although people were beginning to think it old-fashioned. Most of its furniture was by Sheraton. Minnie's diligent polishing with beeswax gave the side tables and chairs a patina that the new furniture would need decades to get.

When Sophie arrived, she stared in astonishment. Luc looked grander than she had ever seen him. His black hair was carefully arranged in the latest *à la Brutus* style, he wore a richly coloured red waistcoat and his shirt was spotless. She knew Lady Theo had dragooned him into going to a tailor. She hadn't expected the results to make him look so handsome.

After she settled herself, Lady Theo had Wynsham, the butler, pour champagne. "For a toast, Sophie love," she explained. "For once, something has gone right. I am now Luc's official guardian. The court approved our petition this morning."

Sophie took a cautious sip of the bubbling wine. It looked better than it tasted and she thought lemonade was much superior. But Luc seemed to like it and drank almost his entire glassful, and he looked happier than Sophie had ever seen him. At least, since they had left Malloryville.

After that shining moment, though, life settled back into a routine that seemed both frustrating and useless. The household's day began early with Lady Theo leaving the house shortly after breakfast for endless meetings with government officials and lawyers. Eighteen minutes later, the carriage arrived back from town with Mr. Lofty, the tutor Lady Theo had hired. Mr. Lofty, or "Toplofty" as Luc immediately nicknamed him, was a nice enough person. In the old days Sophie would have liked him.

"But," she went on after explaining that to Luc, "I don't like learning by ourselves. It's just not as good as school."

"I think it's better. You just don't like it because I won't give you any answers," Luc replied, with a look of mock virtue on his face.

Sophie threw a cushion at him. "It's not only that. You're gone half the time. There's no one to talk to."

That last part was true. Mr. Lofty stayed for lunch, then went back to Montreal. Several minutes later, Luc also left the house and, try as she might, Sophie could never find out exactly what he did with himself. She didn't even know if Lady Theo knew. Luc always managed to come back by the time she returned from the city. To add to Sophie's grievances, she sometimes thought Luc might be spying on Lady Theo. Whenever she was late, so was he.

One afternoon, left by herself and thoroughly bored, Sophie decided she must find out what Luc was doing. He had entirely too many secrets. If he were indeed spying on Lady Theo, they needed to find out. As soon as she could, she would follow him, and to do that, she'd need a disguise.

As she brooded, ideas came fast and furiously. She'd dress as a villager in a homespun dress and hooded cloak, like the women she had seen in Beauharnois. She knew where to buy clothes like that: the market opposite

Rasco's Hotel, where families from the countryside brought goods to sell on Tuesdays and Fridays. All she needed was some excuse to get John Coachman to drive her there.

Her opportunity came earlier than expected. Thursday night Lady Theo announced a short holiday from schoolwork. Mr. Lofty would not come the following day. Splendid, Sophie thought. She'd be able to go to the market. If she was ever going to be able to fool Luc, this would be her best chance.

The following morning, as usual, Lady Theo had left the house before she went down for breakfast. "Where's Luc?" she asked Minnie, the parlour maid. "Has he eaten yet?"

"If he has, it wasn't here," Minnie answered pertly as she began clearing the dishes from the sideboard. "He left even before her ladyship. Will you need anything more, miss?"

Sophie thought if she'd needed another sign, this was it. She could go to the market, buy her clothes, and then hide them by the time Luc returned for lunch. She hurriedly dressed for outdoors, then waited by the back door. When John Coachman returned from driving Lady Theo into Montreal, she dashed over to the coach house just as he began to unharness the horses. "Didn't Lady Theo tell you I needed to go to the market today?"

John Coachman stopped, but kept his hands on the reins. "Why, no, Miss Sophie. She didn't say a word about taking you to the city."

"She must have forgotten. I suspect it's easy, with so much on her mind," Sophie told him, crossing her fingers behind her back. "If we left now, you wouldn't have to harness the horses again."

"There's that," he said in his slow Somerset accent. He and Eloise, Lady Theo's personal maid, had come with her from England and were treated more like friends than servants. Sophie knew that if John even suspected her of lying he'd not only refuse to take her, but tell Lady Theo. He ran his hand over one of the horses after it stamped its feet on the cobbles, then looked at Sophie. "Are you sure, miss? I had the distinct impression she wanted you to stay home today."

"That was during the trial," Sophie told him, again crossing her fingers. "Things have changed now, as you can see. Luc goes off on his own every day. Lady Theo would stop him if there was any danger."

John Coachman rubbed some straw over the horse's back while he thought. "I don't know, miss," he said eventually.

"Please," she said, trying her best to put a beseeching look into her eyes. "I need to get some things, John. It's almost Christmas and, well, I'd like to find something special for Lady Theo and Luc. If I wait until

Lady Theo isn't busy, all the pretty things will be gone. I know they will."

Again, John Coachman tended his horses while he thought. Finally, he tightened the buckles on the harness and gave a dry laugh as he opened the carriage door. "I've never been able to resist blue eyes. Never have and I suppose I never will. Come along."

People thronged the market, and she and John almost had to fight to get in. A raft of smells immediately met them: cured bacon, freshly cooked breads, and pickles of all descriptions. After a while, though, Sophie noticed that few people were buying anything. Most huddled in groups talking quietly. Sophie moved around them, going from stall to stall, with John Coachman hovering about six or seven feet behind her. She bought soft woollen scarves for her papa and Luc, some embroidery silks, and six Irish linen handkerchiefs as a present for Lady Theo. When John collected her packages, she asked if he'd put them in the carriage.

"I can carry them, Miss Sophie. They're not heavy."

Sophie knew that, but she could see a clothes stall about six feet to her left. Somehow she had to rid herself of John, or distract him long enough to be able to buy her dress and cloak. "It's that I need to buy a few more gifts, including one for you. I don't want you to see what I'm giving you. Can you wait for me by the door to St. Paul Street?"

"Miss Sophie! You know my orders. I can't leave you unescorted!"

"Five minutes, John. Nothing can happen to me in five minutes."

"I'm not going to leave you. Her ladyship would have my head if anything happened. What's more, she'd have a good reason to," he replied. He thought for a while, moving her packages from one hand to the other as he did. "Tell you what," he said finally. "I'll move back a little and look the other way. Only for a few moments. It's the best I can do."

After he had moved away grudgingly, Sophie ran back to the counter. She quickly picked out a grey hooded cloak with red embroidery down the sides, a matching dress, and some boots. Adding a red sash to the pile, she asked, "Could you wrap the lot into one parcel and give it to my coachman there, please? That one in the red and gold livery?"

Then she dashed away to the tobacco stall, just a few feet further away. She chose a pipe and a country-man's blend for John.

As she turned to go back to him, a large mob surged into the market from the Notre-Dame Street entrance and blocked her way back. A motley crew, they wore greatcoats of all colours, even the same dark grey

Sophie had seen the soldiers who guarded the governor's house wearing. A few wore top hats, others caps. They clogged the aisles. Every now and then, things would shift and Sophie would see John, fifteen feet or so away, frantically trying to get to her. Then, she'd be carried off in a different direction.

Like most people in the market that day, the newcomers weren't interested in buying. Unlike them, they surged through the aisles, destroying goods at random, absorbing everyone into their wake. Resisting the urge to panic, Sophie did her best to fight the tide, to get to the St. Paul Street entrance. Rasco's, where John had stabled the horses, would then be just across the street. Without bothering to excuse herself for using her elbows, she tried to barge through the crowd. She thought she was making headway until a hand gripped her shoulder and she came to a total stop.

"See what we have here, boys. Look! It's that little miss from the court," said a voice she remembered, and had hoped never to hear again.

Alf! In court, she'd thought him fat and obnoxious. Now, however, he seemed a refuge as he stared at her with a worried look on his face. "You shouldn't be by yourself, miss. Not today."

"I'm not by myself," Sophie said, looking desperately around, searching for John Coachman.

Alf appeared to do the same. "Can't see any of your friends, miss. Tell you what, though. You come to the dance with us. We'll look after you. You don't want to be caught up with the likes of him." Just in time, he pulled her aside as a slab of beef hurtled towards them. He pointed to the man who had thrown it. Obviously, he was part of the group going through the market and destroying anything they thought might belong to the French-speaking farmers. Sophie watched in silent anger as they threw even salted fish from Boston against the back wall.

"Ought to be a law about things like that. Spoiling good food. No matter what, shouldn't spoil food," Alf muttered, then looked at Sophie again. "Now, you come with me, miss. We'll go to the dance together. I'll look after you."

Although she should have found him menacing, Sophie believed he meant well. His words didn't make much sense, though. She had never heard of people dancing this early. She tried to resist, as Alf and his friends walked towards the Notre-Dame exit, but she wasn't strong enough. As she struggled to free herself from his grasp, she looked for John. Finally, Alf stopped and looked down at her.

"I can't go with you. You're going the wrong way," she told him. "I'm supposed to meet my coachman at the other door."

"You won't have much chance of that. Not with this crowd."

Sophie had heard stories about undertows, the currents in the sea that sucked people in and sent them every which way. She felt as though she were caught in one. She had no chance of escaping the current heading out of the market through the Notre-Dame Street doors. To her surprise, Alf's hand on her shoulders was gentle as he protected her from being buffeted by the flotsam and jetsam around her.

She looked one last time for John Coachman. It was futile. She was walled in by a solid mass of people. Where they went, so did she. This time when Alf moved, she didn't fight him. She just allowed the crowd to take her where it went and reserved her strength for later. Although she could see little, she knew the exact moment they left the market. The air was just that much crisper and she rubbed her hands tightly within her muff to warm them.

The mob marched almost with military precision to the cadence of a drum. Someone up ahead started singing, his voice strong enough to be heard by the hundreds of people:

O, the twitching dance, the twitching dance,
I want to go to the twitching dance.
See 'em dangle,

Their legs a-tangle,
Yes, I want to go to the twitching dance.

The song had a catchy tune. Soon everyone sang as they swung along, the fresh snow crunching beneath their feet. Sophie sang as well, once she'd picked up the words and tune. She felt uneasy, though. The crowd sounded happy, yet she sensed a strange savagery in it. To avoid being trampled, Sophie had to almost run to keep up with them. Every step took her further and further away from John Coachman and Rasco's. She knew that. Yet, she didn't see any alternative, except to stay close to Alf. She felt she could trust him.

She held her nose as they passed Mr. Molson's brewery. She never had liked the smell of hops. Alf joked with his friends about stopping there on the way back to town. About ten minutes later, ripples of excitement spread throughout the crowd, and Sophie caught a glimpse of a huge stone wall.

"Here we are, missy," Alf said. Then he lifted her effortlessly atop his shoulders. "This will give you the best view."

From her vantage point, Sophie could see in all directions. The twin spires of Notre-Dame Cathedral dominated the skyline behind her in the far distance. To the right, the partially frozen St. Lawrence wended its way sluggishly towards the Atlantic Ocean. Behind the stone walls to Sophie's left was an intimidating building, at least two hundred feet high.

The crowd wasn't interested in the building. It surged towards the gates. Behind them, a large, newly built wooden structure could be seen. For a while, Sophie couldn't see much detail, but when Alf turned, she saw two ropes attached to the top beam and suddenly understood everything about the morning.

Alf and his friends were not going to a dance. The "twitching dance" would be a hanging. Sophie started trying to wriggle her way off Alf's shoulders. She did not want to see two men suffocate to death when those ropes tightened around their necks and cut off their air. "Alf! Mr. Alf!" she called desperately. "Let me down!"

Alf swung her down to the ground immediately. "What's the matter, missy?"

Sophie tried to think of a way to explain why she had to get away from the crowd, a way he would understand. She looked around the crowd for inspiration and frowned when she saw a solitary priest's hat on the opposite side of the road. Why should he be by himself? Usually she saw priests on the streets in pairs. Maybe, she shrugged, he had been caught up in the mob just like she had been.

It was strange, though. People within the mob changed places. They didn't march in set order as soldiers. Sometimes a person sped up just as another slowed down. Now, as people jostled for a better view, the priest managed to keep the same distance from Alf.

Then, almost as though he felt her studying him, he turned his head slightly. Sophie gasped as she recognized Bart. She felt stupid. She should have remembered this was how he disguised himself. Though why he should be in a mob going to watch a hanging boggled her mind. Thoughts of being kidnapped again raced through her head, and she looked around, half-expecting to see the two men in the blue suits who had tried to kidnap her a few weeks earlier. As though he had an extra sense that warned him he'd been recognized, Bart began fighting his way across to her.

Sophie looked on the ground for fresh horse droppings for manure balls. Then, with Bart only about six feet away, she tugged on Alf's arm. "Help me ... please!" she shouted, doing her best to be heard over the mob's hubbub.

"Help you? How?"

"See that priest? He's been, um, bothering me."

Her words had an immediate effect. An even better one than she'd hoped. Alf's hands bunched into fists. His eyes narrowed into slits as he stared at Bart.

"I'll fix him."

"No!" Sophie said immediately. After seeing Alf's surprised look she went on, "If you could just help me get away from here, help me to get back to the market, I should be safe. I can get home from there."

"You'd be better off letting me take care of him here. That way, you won't have to keep looking over your shoulder."

Sophie shuddered. "I just want to get home."

"You shouldn't be out by yourself, even to see the dance," Alf commented, returning to an old theme as he began battling his way backwards.

It was slow going. Part of the problem was that they had to go through the mob head-on. Not surprisingly, Bart made better progress, even with his limp, than they did.

"It's no use. He's going to get me," Sophie said despairingly.

"No, he's not," Alf told her, putting himself between her and Bart. "I'm sorry, miss. I didn't quite believe you," he went on, his voice showing surprise. "He really *is* after you. Priests shouldn't bother young ladies. I don't care what religion they are."

To Sophie's astonishment, he picked her up and tossed her free of the crowd. She stumbled and, as she tried to get her balance, Alf turned back into Bart's path. Before Bart could say anything, Alf swung his fist in a haymaker, right into his face. As Sophie watched, half-admiringly, half-horrified, Bart stopped in his tracks as blood gushed from his nose. He raised a hand feebly, then toppled over like a dead tree in a windstorm.

Sophie took one last, horrified look at him before turning to her protector. "Thank you, Mr. Alf. Thank you."

Then, she ran. Not towards Bart, but back towards the market. Back towards Rasco's, to John Coachman, to safety.

CHAPTER TEN

Sophie knew she had to tell Lady Theo about her adventure. For all kinds of reasons. One, of course, was self-preservation. If she didn't admit to going to the market and almost getting lost, John Coachman would certainly regale her ladyship's ears with the tale. He'd told her that he'd aged ten years that morning.

Once Sophie had a little time to think about her morning, she realized that Bart must have followed her. It was just too much of a coincidence, otherwise. Why would he have been part of that mob if it hadn't been for her?

She waited impatiently for Luc to return. She wanted to know what he thought about it. She wouldn't tell him why she had cajoled John into driving her to the market, of course. She'd use the Christmas present excuse. And she'd ask Luc what he meant when he said that Bert and Bart must have an important reason to want her back in Malloryville so badly.

But when Luc blundered into the house, his face was white and pinched. He looked at her, then stumbled his way upstairs to his room. Minutes later, she heard him vomiting. He stayed in his bedroom, refusing to open the door, even for the housekeeper. Every now and then, Sophie heard him retching. She was relieved when Lady Theo returned.

"Luc needs a doctor. He's sick, Lady Theo. Really sick," Sophie announced as soon as she walked through the front door.

"A doctor won't help him, Sophie."

"Why ever not?"

Lady Theo stood for a moment, warming her hands by the fire. Her face looked grimmer than usual and, as she stood lost in thought, she seemed unapproachable. Finally, she looked across the room to Sophie and sighed. "Because he's not really sick."

"But he is," Sophie argued vehemently. "You don't know anything, anymore. You're always dashing off to some meeting or other. But Luc's really sick. I've heard him cast up his accounts four or five times. Maybe he's got cholera."

Before Lady Theo could answer, Minnie, the new parlour maid, bustled in with the tea tray. After she had set it down, Lady Theo waved her from the room.

"We'll pour it ourselves, Minnie. Thank you." Then she beckoned to Sophie. "Come over here. By the fire, child. And pour me a cup, will you? It's been a trying day. I'm exhausted."

For several minutes the two sipped their tea in silence. Eventually Lady Theo seemed to come to some sort of decision. She sighed and ruffled Sophie's curls. "You're right. It must seem as though I've deserted you and it's long past time where we talked about everything to do with your father. But first, you have to understand that today's been a very hard one for Luc, dear. He saw something dreadful happen and his stomach's trying to get the memory of it out of his system. That's why he's sick."

"What happened?" Sophie asked, thinking back to the hanging she'd almost witnessed.

Before she could answer, the door opened and Luc walked in. He took a quick look at the plump scones, the cream and jam, for once in his life shuddering at the sight of delicious food. Nevertheless, Lady Theo poured him a cup of tea and stirred a couple of teaspoons of sugar into it. "Drink it," she ordered as she handed it to him. "It will do you good."

Luc took the cup. It trembled in his hand and Sophie could see the tea sloshing from one side to the other. "I don't feel like putting anything British into my system today," he finally muttered.

"Don't be silly, Luc. Tea's tea."

Luc slammed the delicate cup back onto the table with a crash. "And are British British?" he said angrily. "Are you the same as those men this morning? The soldiers?"

Lady Theo also put her cup back on the table as she faced Luc. "Yes, Luc, I'm English. Or British, as you'd say here. Am I the same as those soldiers you saw this morning? Of course. I'm as loyal to Queen Victoria as they are. They were just doing their job. In other ways, though, I'm different. You have to know that, otherwise you'd never ask the question." Then to Sophie's astonishment, she seemed to attack Luc by asking, "What about you, Luc? Are you as Canadian as those poor rebels?"

Luc glared at her. For one moment Sophie thought he would either throw his teacup at Lady Theo or storm out of the house. Again, she felt left out. She could understand their words but had no idea what they were talking about. But before she could say anything, Luc put his head between his hands and started to sob. It was heartbreaking to listen to him and just when Sophie felt she couldn't bear it any longer, he began to talk, rapidly and convulsively.

"That's just it. And you know it. Me, I'm neither fish nor fowl. Neither Canadian nor British. Canadian father, British mother. And it's only because you let me live here that I'm not in prison or even dead. Like poor Joseph." He buried his face in his hands again and wept.

Eventually, he hunched back against the sofa's cushions as though he could hide in them. For some minutes only an occasional sob broke the silence. Then Lady Theo walked across the room and sat next to Luc. After a second's hesitation, he put his arms around her and allowed himself to be rocked like a baby.

Sophie looked at the pair of them feeling jealous. After all, she was the one whose father was in a jail somewhere, although no one knew where. She was also the one in a foreign country where she knew no one and in which she had almost been kidnapped. Again. But when she looked at Lady Theo's face and saw Luc's pain reflected in it, she knew something terrible indeed must have happened.

"Tell me what you're talking about," she begged. "Who is Joseph?"

"Was," Luc answered sharply. "Joseph *was* Joseph Duquette. You saw him at his trial. He was Mr. Cardinal's student. Remember?"

"Of course, I remember."

"Well," he continued. "Joseph was a friend of Marc's. He was always at our house. And today...." He gulped, and for a few minutes Sophie thought he might never finish his sentence. But eventually he pulled himself away from Lady Theo, dried his eyes, and faced her.

"Sophie, they hanged the first men. This morning. Mr. Cardinal and Joseph. Joseph Duquette. Only them, though. I went in case something went wrong. I thought they might decide to include Marc at the last moment and not tell me."

Sophie felt weird. She wanted to tell Luc that she understood, that she had almost seen the hangings herself, but she was too scared of Lady Theo's reaction to just blurt it out. In her anxiety, she began singing and both Luc and Lady Theo stared in astonishment:

O, the twitching dance, the twitching dance,
I want to go to the twitching dance.
See 'em dangle,
Their legs a-tangle,
Yes, I want to go to the twitching dance.

"Where on earth did you learn that?" Luc immediately demanded, fists bunched and eyes angry. "That's a song the English made up to taunt us."

Lady Theo waved her hand, almost knocking her teacup into Sophie's lap. "That doesn't matter right now, Luc. You have to put your mind to rest. That's the important thing. They will tell you if Marc is going to be hanged, God forbid. They have to let you know at least a couple of days in advance so you can say your goodbyes. They have to. It's the law."

Luc looked at Lady Theo and Sophie saw a deep distrust in his eyes. "It seems to me the law's only kept in this province when it's convenient," he said scathingly. "There wasn't anything legal about Marc's conviction, was there? They didn't prove their case against him. Everyone knew that magistrate lied. He's the one who should be in jail, not Marc."

"I agree they didn't prove that Marc was guilty."

His one-shouldered shrug showed his opinion of Lady Theo's reply. "They didn't care. They'd made up their minds beforehand."

Sophie wanted to walk out of the room. She hated arguments. She particularly hated the fact that two of the three people she cared most about in the world were having this particular one. She imagined hundreds of people marching down St. Mary's Street towards the jail with jugs of cider and brandy and singing "The Twitching Song," only instead of anticipating the deaths of Mr. Cardinal or Joseph, the revellers in this imaginary scene were celebrating the hanging of her papa.

"Stop it," she implored Luc. "Arguing with Lady Theo won't help anything."

Luc couldn't imagine her thoughts, of course. Caught up in his argument, he turned to Lady Theo and asked scornfully, "Aren't they supposed to let you know where Sophie's papa is? Tell her I'm right."

The sadness in Lady Theo's eyes deepened. "Yes, of course you're right. Normally, they'd have to tell me. But right now, as long as Lower Canada's under martial law, the law means only what the government wants. But it won't last, Luc. Don't give up hope. Sir John's truly not a bloodthirsty monster."

"Then why wasn't Joseph pardoned? Why did they let him suffer like they did?" Luc seemed to look at a picture in the far distance. For several moments, Sophie thought he wasn't going to talk anymore.

Then he continued, his voice gentle and so different from the harsh jeering tone he'd used when arguing with Lady Theo. "It was so horrible. Joseph's left arm was deformed. Somehow they didn't tie the rope tightly enough around it, or something. When they opened the trap door in the gallows, he managed to grab hold of one of the posts with it. That kept him from dropping down like poor Mr. Cardinal did."

"You saw this? You watched them die?" Sophie asked, suddenly grateful for Bart. If she hadn't seen him, she might not have had the impetus to break free of the crowd. Then, she would have had to stand next to Alf and watch two men die.

"That's what was so horrible," Luc answered, his eyes seemingly fixed on the gruesome picture. "Joseph kept swinging against the post, smashing his head against it again and again until blood covered all his face.

133

All the time, he kept swinging and swinging against the post. Swinging and struggling to free himself."

Both Sophie and Lady Theo shuddered at the horrific description. Luc rocked back against the sofa, again staring into the distance. His voice was strained and even softer when he went on. "After a while, everyone in the crowd began shouting for a pardon. Sometimes, in the old days, if something like that happened, they'd think it was a sign from God and free the person. So, people kept shouting, 'Free him! Free him!' I thought we'd succeeded when the captain, who was in charge of the hanging, came over. He talked to the soldiers and they cut Joseph down. Everyone cheered. I felt so happy for Marc. I thought God had really heard my prayers and was letting me know by this miracle that Marc wouldn't hang either. I was so happy."

Lady Theo seemed to know that it wasn't the story's end because she took Luc into her arms again as though he were a little boy and tucked his head under her chin and just held him tightly. Eventually, Luc pulled away. When he began talking again, the words came out in a desperate rush, as though he couldn't bear to even talk about the morning more than he had to.

"They took the blindfold off and put a new one on. Then they made Joseph climb the stairs again, and this time, when they tied him up, they took extra care and made sure both arms were tightly bound. Then they dropped the trapdoor again and ..."

Sophie crept over to Lady Theo and pushed herself into her arms. Lady Theo reached over and pulled Luc towards herself as well and the three of them sat there crying for a young man who had died because he had tried to borrow guns to help in a rebellion. After a while, they stopped crying for Joseph Duquette and for Mr. Cardinal, and cried for themselves and for the fact that they didn't know if fate would decree that Benjamin Mallory and Marc Moriset would also climb the gallows' stairs and meet their ends when its trapdoor dropped open.

CHAPTER ELEVEN

Life in the household changed yet again after that evening. Luc would do his schoolwork with a fierce eagerness, then leave the house. Sophie never followed him. Her experiences on the day of the hanging had taught her to be wary. As well, she didn't have much free time because Lady Theo began to entertain. Mostly that meant she was "at home" for a couple of afternoons when she and Sophie received callers in the drawing room and talked about fashions and the latest news from London.

Sophie thought these "at homes" a total waste of time, until Lady Theo told her they might have to rely on some of their callers to sign petitions to free her papa — that is, once they'd found out where he was. So, she began to look upon the afternoon social duties as a kind of work, something that was just as important as whatever Luc was doing to free his brother. When she told him this, he snorted in disgust.

"It's nothing but ladies' work, Sophie. Sipping tea out of china cups. You're the St. Lawrence Suburb of Montreal Ladies' Tea Society. Me? I'm ferreting out bits of information. A bit here, a bit there. It's real work."

"Then, what have you found out about Papa?"

He looked crestfallen. "He's not in Napierville. I know that. He hasn't been there for weeks. It's like he disappeared. Nobody I've talked with knows anything. But I found out one thing about your brother Clart. The last time anyone saw him, he was running towards the border during the Battle of Lacolle as fast as he could. Stampeding horses would not have caught him. He didn't stay to fight honourably, Sophie. He ran away in the middle of the battle. Ran when we still had a chance to win."

That sounded like Clart, Sophie thought. He had charm, great plans, but always squirmed out of things at the slightest sign of trouble. Still, she wondered where he was. If Luc's story was true, maybe he was in the United States. Yet, obviously he wasn't in Malloryville. No wonder Bert and Bart were so concerned.

When she told Lady Theo this later that evening, she didn't seem terribly surprised. "I'd heard something along the same lines, dear. But I agree; it's strange. It's as though he has disappeared off the face of the earth."

"Perhaps he's dead," Sophie said glumly.

"I don't think so." Luc interjected. "If he is, he didn't die in Canada. Most families have taken their loved ones from the morgues by now. Of course, there are a few bodies that no one's identified. Somebody from Vermont has looked at all of them, though. Your brothers probably sent him to make sure. At least, that's what I heard."

About a week later, Luc rushed into the front parlour. A look of comical dismay appeared on his face when he seemed to realize that he'd inadvertently joined the St. Lawrence Suburb of Montreal Ladies' Tea Society. He hastily made his bow, then perched nervously on the edge of his chair. Sophie almost laughed aloud when she looked at him. His body was a mass of quivering nerves and, judging by the expression on his face, he wished he were elsewhere.

He couldn't leave the room, though. Two of the ladies in it belonged to the Montreal Benevolent Society, which Sophie knew his grandmother subscribed to. While she poured the tea, Luc politely handed around Cook's best scones and discussed his grandmother's health. Then he sat once more on the edge of a chair and fidgeted until the ladies left.

He let out a sigh of relief almost immediately. "I thought they'd never go."

"You didn't have to drink tea with them," Sophie retorted. "I had two cups."

"Children," Lady Theo chided. "Don't you know who they were, Luc?"

"The president and vice president of the Ladies' Benevolent Society," he replied.

"The vice president just happens to be married to the attorney general of this province," Lady Theo told him. "Her husband is Sir John's right-hand man. He will help decide which prisoners should be hanged or pardoned, so I'm very glad you watched your manners. When Marc Moriset's name comes up, Mrs. Ogden just might say, 'Oh, that's Luc's older brother. Luc's such a polite young man. I'm sure Marc must have been led astray. The Morisets are such a nice family.'"

"I'd hate to be him," Sophie blurted out. Then, seeing their looks of puzzlement, added, "Mr. Ogden, that is. Having to decide which men die, which ones get out of jail. It would be horrible having to make those decisions."

Her words had a strange effect on Luc. He smacked his head and exclaimed, "I almost forgot to tell you! The tea must have gone to my head. I have to tell you why I came home early. I think I know where Mr. Mallory is."

"What?" Lady Theo and Sophie exclaimed simultaneously.

Luc grinned and almost pranced around the room. He stopped by the fireplace and picked up one of the

Staffordshire dogs on the mantelpiece. When he put it back and patted it, Sophie would have sworn he had an identical look of smugness on his face. "Tell us," she exhorted. "Don't stand there grinning and dancing around like a maniac."

When he began speaking, his words tumbled out in a torrent. "One of my friends heard a rumour a couple of weeks ago about an Englishman in the infirmary at Fort St. John. He didn't think anything about it. Where else would a sick Englishman go, after all? Then he heard there was a guard at his door. The soldiers told everyone it was because he was infectious."

"They wanted to make sure he didn't spread it," Sophie said impatiently. "Go on."

"Well, you're right. It made sense. My friend didn't think much more about it. He didn't tell me because I was asking about prisoners in jail, and in Napierville. But people started talking about him because the army had brought him there in the dead of night. That seemed a little strange."

"Not if he took sick in the middle of the night," Lady Theo said dryly, sounding disappointed.

"Well, the man seems to have recovered. People have seen him walking around the grounds. Under escort, though. And there's more: his only visitor is the main interrogator in the Napierville area. So, my friend wonders why he comes so often to see a man with a contagious disease. When he thinks further, he wonders if this is where the government might have hidden Mr. Mallory."

Sophie looked at Lady Theo. "Do you think it's Papa? I'd be sorry if he's sick, but it would feel so good to know where he was. I wouldn't have nightmares about him being dead somewhere."

Lady Theo looked thoughtful. "How much do you trust your friend, Luc?"

"A lot."

"I want it to be true so badly," she said, rubbing her temple in a rare display of exhaustion. "Part of me says it must be Benjamin. We've looked everywhere else and we know the government's hidden him away someplace. And what better place could there be? A hospital in an army fort?"

"What do we do?" Sophie asked.

"I'll ask Mr. Christie for tea tomorrow. I think he'll be able to give us impartial advice. I don't trust my lawyers. I think they're too scared of how the government might retaliate if they helped me fight properly."

Dinner that night was semi-celebratory. Cook had made Luc's favourite plum-duff dessert and a delicate syllabub for Sophie. Afterwards, Lady Theo challenged both of them to a game of spillikins, adding, "I can beat both of you with one hand tied behind my back."

That was probably true, Sophie thought, as the piece of wood she was trying to tease out of the pile hit another stick. It trembled, and she thought she was safe for a while, but then it crashed into the pile. "You're out," Luc said, announcing the obvious with glee. "My turn."

He proved to be remarkably dextrous and had eliminated half the remaining sticks when they heard a knock on the front door. A minute or so later, Wynsham reported that he had ushered a young man into the front parlour. "A Lieutenant Daultry, my lady. He says he has urgent business with you."

Luc paled, obviously thinking it had something to do with Marc. "May I see him as well?"

"Me too," Sophie begged.

"Make sure he has a glass of sherry. Or whatever he prefers, Wynsham. Tell him that I'll be along presently."

After the butler left, she sat in thought. "Luc," she said eventually, "I don't think this has anything to do with Marc. If they had decided his fate, I'm sure it would be the sheriff's officer who would serve notice on you. I think I'll see what this Lieutenant Daultry wants myself." Almost absent-mindedly she made a new spillikins pile. "Have a tournament," Lady Theo suggested, moving towards the door, spitting out orders as she went. "Take turns. Each of you takes only one stick out, then it's the other's turn. I'll have a special treat for the winner."

When she returned a few minutes later, they hadn't finished the game. But Lady Theo seemed unconcerned. She walked to her chair by the fire, stared at a letter, then put her head in her hands.

Sophie and Luc looked at each other, both clearly frightened. They had never seen Lady Theo so distraught before. "What is it?" they clamoured. "Bad news?"

Wynsham entered the room with a glass of brandy on a silver tray. "Drink this, my lady. You'll find it will help."

The fact that Lady Theo drank some of it frightened Sophie more than anything. "What's happened?"

Lady Theo made a strange strangled sound — a half sob, half laugh. "It's your father, dear. We've found him at last. My friend Charles Grey sent this dispatch. He's been seriously injured and is being looked after by the Sisters of Charity in Châteauguay. Charles wants me to meet him there tomorrow."

"In Châteauguay? The Grey Nuns took him in? Why didn't they let anyone know?" Luc demanded.

"Apparently, that was the army's fault. The only way it allowed them to nurse Benjamin. They had to swear to keep his whereabouts a secret."

Sophie clutched Lady Theo's hand. "It's true? It's really Papa?"

"Yes, child. It's really your papa. Charles is an old friend of both of us. He wouldn't play us false."

"But he says Papa's been hurt. Is he better now?"

Lady Theo didn't answer immediately. She looked at the letter again, frowning as she did. "Charles says that most of his wounds are healed," she said carefully.

During her days in the packed courtroom, Sophie had learned to listen. Now she clearly heard what Theo wasn't saying. "Most? He's still sick?"

"He's almost better," Lady Theo replied. "Now," she went on as she stood, "I have to make preparations. Lieutenant Daultry's returning for me early in the morning. I'll see your papa in the afternoon and probably stay the night in Châteauguay. Listen carefully, Luc. There's to be no gallivanting around until I get back. You stay with Sophie. If you need anything from the city, send John Coachman for it. Understand?"

"I understand," Luc answered.

"And you'll do what I said?" Lady Theo went on, looking Luc straight in the eye. "I want your word of honour on this, Luc. Do I have it?"

"Yes, my lady. I promise I will look after Sophie."

Sophie didn't know whether she should be offended by this or not. On one hand, she wanted to tell Lady Theo she could look after herself. On the other hand, she now knew that wasn't so. She had needed Alf's help the last time she'd ventured out by herself. In many ways, Montreal was still a strange city to her. Then thoughts of her papa flooded her mind as she wondered what she could send with Lady Theo that would cheer him up. "I'm going to write a letter," she announced. "You'll give it to Papa for me, won't you?"

"You know I will," Lady Theo told her. "Bring it to my room before you go to bed."

The time waiting for Charles Grey to return seemed an eternity. Benjamin, now aware of the vastness of his memory loss, hoped that Charles could fill in more than a few empty spaces. He treasured each clear picture in his mind as if it were the most precious silk from China — the loons diving into the lake, the times he had spent shooting quail with Charles — and longed for more.

He fretted as well about his convalescence, sensing that he had once been an active man. "I'm not used to sitting around and doing nothing," he complained to Sister Marie-Josephte.

"Then what did you do, monsieur?" she asked in reply.

"I don't know," he answered unhappily.

He thought his time with her might be coming to an end. He had almost recovered from his wounds and he desperately wanted to explore the world beyond the confines of the small hospital ward in the nuns' house. "If I left," he said one afternoon, "some of my memories might return. Somebody or something might make me remember more. I think I should start walking around outside, at the very least."

"C'est impossible, monsieur," Soeur Marie-Josephte replied.

"Why?"

"The Colonel will explain," she told him, then refused to say more.

She was, however, quite willing to tell him why he had been given into her care. "In the Hôtel Dieu, our hospital in Montreal," she told him, "I was the one who knew the lunatics. The ones with problems in their minds. I have nursed men like you before."

"Do you think I'll ever get better?" he asked immediately.

She took a long time with her tatting before she answering, cutting and tying threads, tidying her bobbin basket. "That, monsieur, is in the hands of the good Lord. I think you will get most of your mind back. Not all, probably. Console yourself with the thought, though, that you are not the worst patient I've had. One poor man couldn't even remember how to eat properly. We had to teach him how to use a knife and fork. You? You kept all those memories. It's only people you have forgotten."

"I remembered Colonel Grey."

"But not your wife? Are you married, monsieur? And children? Do you have ten? One? How many?"

Benjamin slumped back against the pillow in disgust. He hadn't even thought to ask himself such elemental questions. To make matters worse, the familiar thud of boots sounded in the hallway. He closed his eyes, in no mood to deal with the arrogant captain who visited every afternoon.

It was a different story when he heard Charles Grey's voice a few days later. He walked towards the door eagerly, only to stop dead in his tracks at the sight of one of the most beautiful women he'd ever seen. Of greater significance, she was also someone he remembered.

"My lady," he said before he smiled and bowed. He straightened and walked towards her, his hand outstretched. "What are you doing here? The last time I saw you was at the Duke of Devonshire's ball. You were waltzing with Charles. I envied him then, as I do now. Permit me to introduce myself. I'm Benjamin Mallory of ..."

For a few seconds he had a picture of a huge house in a magnificent part of London. He could see a carriage standing in front of it with its coachman and groom in gold and blue livery. A white-haired butler stood in the open doorway and he almost completed his sentence by saying "Grosvenor Square." Then, images of a small town set amongst towering mountains flooded his mind. He saw a couple of mills built near the mouth of a mountain stream and almost heard the sound of iron gears turning. A road went west from the mills and he knew that if he walked that road he'd reach his home.

"Malloryville!" he said triumphantly. "I'm Benjamin Mallory of Malloryville in the state of Vermont."

Elated by his success, he didn't notice, at first, the effect his words had on his listeners. Only when he heard a gasp from Charles Grey and saw the lady sag in his arms did he realize that something was seriously wrong. He stepped forward immediately. "Here, Charles. Here's a chair. Would she like to sit down? Can the sisters bring anything?" he asked.

"Some tea, I think," the Colonel responded. "She's had a shock."

Sister Marie-Josephte left the room. Benjamin watched as Charles carefully helped the lady to a chair, perturbed by the paleness of her cheeks. He sensed a fragility that had not been there when she had entered the room. He hovered by the chair, wondering what else he could do.

"Benjamin, stop fretting. You're making me nervous. Now, stand still and allow me to present my dear friend, Lady Theodosia Thornleigh."

Benjamin bowed again and Lady Theodosia took his hand, holding on to it with a desperation he didn't understand. He also didn't know why his pulse suddenly raced or why the blackness that was so familiar seemed just a little lighter.

"Now," the Colonel continued, "let's get acquainted and try to work out what to do with you."

CHAPTER TWELVE

The following morning Sophie sat at the library table writing an essay on the Boston Tea Party. Across the table from her, Luc muttered to himself as he laboriously translated a passage from Thucydides into English. "I hate ancient Greek," he grumbled, after slamming his dictionary on the table. "I don't see why I have to learn it. No one speaks it any more. Not even the real Greeks. Who cares about the Peloponnesian War, anyway?"

Sophie grinned at him, enjoying his frustration. "I used to think about French that way."

"French is different," Luc replied in a superior tone. "Everyone knows it's the universal language of the world. But ancient Greek? Nobody's had a conversation in it for two thousand years. Why should I learn it? I didn't have to at my old school."

"You learned Latin, though," Sophie pointed out. "Nobody speaks that today."

"The priests do. When I go to Marc's church, everything's in Latin."

Sophie couldn't think of a clever retort so they both returned to their homework until she yawned and stretched. "I'm finished. At least I knew what to write about for a change. My grandfather used to talk about the Boston Tea Party. All the time. It was something I couldn't help knowing about."

"Well, Toplofty sees things quite differently from your grandfather. I hope you remember that. Don't forget he thinks your grandfather was a rebel, not a patriot."

Sophie wandered over to the wall of books, looking for something interesting to read, while Luc finished Thucydides. "It's strange, how things turn out," she replied as she gently blew the dust off an old leather-bound book. "Grandpapa and his best friend, Sam Adams, are heroes. Only because they won, though. If they'd lost their rebellion, they might have been put into prison, like Marc."

"That's right," Luc told her with a wry smile. "On the other hand, your grandfather could have been hanged. Just think how different the world would have been with no Sophie Mallory in it."

She hadn't thought of that and now her worries about Papa flooded back. "Luc.... Could Papa really be as close as Châteauguay? Why didn't we know about it?"

Luc stopped writing and put his pen carefully into the inkstand. "Because we never looked there. I only asked my friends about jails in Napierville and Montreal. That's where Lady Theo sent her investigators, as well. Everyone told us your papa was captured at Lacolle, near the border, then taken to Napierville. Not one person mentioned Châteauguay."

"Well, I'd like to know how he ended up there. He wasn't part of the rebellion. He wasn't fighting anyone, so how did he get injured? It doesn't make sense."

"You ..." Luc began, then obviously changed his mind about answering. He snapped his books shut with a flourish as he changed the subject. "That's it. I'm finished. Thank goodness — it's almost time for elevenses. Want to play something while we wait?"

Sophie, after looking at the expression on Luc's face, decided not to question him further. By now she'd learned to understand some of his expressions. When he closed his lips tightly, questions became a waste of time. "Sure. Anything's better than just sitting around. Span counters with cards?"

After Luc fetched a fresh pack, they flipped their cards in turn towards the wall, trying to get them as close to it as possible without touching the other's cards. Sophie's aim was usually erratic but when she flicked her last card so that it landed perfectly, she laughed in delight. "I've won. Finally, I've done something right. Loser gets to pick up the cards."

Luc pulled on the bell strap. Within minutes, Minnie brought steaming mugs of cocoa and a plate with slices of cake. They munched contentedly for a few minutes, then Luc watched as Sophie packed up the cards they'd been playing with. "What do you think of Minnie?" he asked.

Sophie stopped stuffing the cards back into their box. "Think about Minnie? I don't. What do you mean?"

"I don't know. It's a feeling. We don't really need her, you know. There's not enough work unless Lady Theo wants to entertain every night. Sometimes I think Wynsham took one look at her pretty face and decided to hire her as a kind of ornament."

"You think she's pretty?"

"Of course she is," Luc replied. "Are you saying you hadn't noticed?"

Sophie truly hadn't noticed and she felt a little ashamed. Her papa made a point of knowing all his servants. Now, she worried that she'd become like a few people she'd met in England who thought servants were nothing but animated sticks of furniture. Rather than admit this, however, she asked another obvious question. "Why are you so interested in her anyway?"

Luc pointed his finger at her and wagged it. "Not for the reason you think," he said immediately. "There's something about her that worries me. She was in my room yesterday, going through my things, and I'd bet she was in yours as well. And she's always in the hallway when we go out. We must have the best-polished hallway tables in the entire city."

"And banisters," Sophie added. "She's always polishing the front staircase, as well."

Luc rocked a little in his armchair. "I think her reason for coming to see if there was work here was nothing more than an excuse. I think she's a spy."

"She's a woman," Sophie blurted out in surprise.

"Women can be spies," Luc told her bitterly. "Marc says they're always the best ones. Maybe that's why I'm wondering about Minnie."

Sophie didn't know what to think. Marc's comment made a lot of sense, though. Women always seemed to know what was going on. She told Luc this, adding, "That's probably why Lady Theo makes sure she keeps in touch with everyone she knows. She's always saying you never know who can help Papa. I suppose that's what Marc means."

To her surprise, Luc laughed. "I'm sure he had something quite different in mind."

Later, when she was saying her prayers, Sophie thought back to that conversation. It seemed ridiculous that the government should send a spy to their house. What could it possibly hope to find out? Who would Minnie be spying on? Lady Theo? Luc? Sophie shuddered and when she resumed her prayers and prayed for protection "from all perils and dangers," the phrase had especial meaning for her.

A messenger arrived the next day with a letter from Lady Theo. Papa, she told Sophie, had not recovered fully and she needed to stay a few more days to work out how best to help him. She would let them know when she would be home.

"I don't like it. There's something more than she's telling us," Sophie announced, handing the letter over to Luc.

"I don't like it either. It means I have to stick around the house for a few more days. I could be skating on the lake or sledding down Mount Royal. Instead, I'm penned up here with you until she gets back."

"If it's so horrible, why not go skating or sledding?"

"Because I promised on my honour." Luc ground the words out between compressed lips. "It's not really the skating or sledding that I'll miss the most. I won't be able to see Marc. I promised I'd take him some more blankets. He says he's close to freezing some nights."

Sophie hadn't worried much about Marc in the last couple of days. Somehow, she'd come to assume that he would escape hanging and be set free. "Is it really bad in jail?"

"Marc's lucky, sort of. He's had his trial and knows its outcome. He knows we're working to save him. He's also much richer than most of the other prisoners. He eats pretty well. He's also able to buy enough extra food for the other men in his cell. The nuns help as well. They always try to make sure that everyone has enough to eat. But you know how it goes," he said, shrugging philosophically. "He gives the jailer a dollar. Suddenly, there's hot water for a bath or for shaving. No dollar, no hot water. It's the way the world works."

Sophie looked at him in dismay. "I hadn't realized it was like that. I thought they had to give them food and everything."

Luc grimaced. "He's given a room with stone walls and a stone floor. He gets bread twice a day, and water. Of course, the water's frozen most of the time. Everything else is a luxury. Only men with relatives willing to pay get anything extra. Like blankets."

Sophie walked out of the room slowly, wondering what she could do to help. She could knit socks and mufflers, she thought, and she had just started up the stairs to find some yarn when Minnie told her that Wynsham needed her in the front parlour.

He stood at the doorway, a piece of blue paper in his hand, glaring at a man in a dark uniform. "Miss

Sophie. This, ahem, *individual* needs to see you," he declared, his nostrils flaring in disgust.

"Me?" Sophie asked in a voice that trembled. The man reminded her of the men in blue suits who had tried to kidnap her a month earlier.

"If you are Miss Sophie Mallory," the man replied. He had a low, gravelly voice that Sophie found intimidating. She wished Luc was around. Or, better still, Alf with his haymaker punch.

Nevertheless, she faced the man and the time spent having manners pounded into her became worthwhile. "I am Miss Mallory," she replied, with dignity.

"Well, then, my job's easy. This is a summons, Miss Mallory. You are to be in court tomorrow so that a judge can appoint a guardian for you. At ten o'clock. Do you understand?"

Sophie stared at him. "I'm to go to court by myself?"

The man smiled. "Not to worry, little miss. I hear your brother has come all the way up from Vermont to make sure you are not alone."

Sophie felt like fainting. But, she chided herself, how could she do something so foolish. She had survived a rebellion, survived being taken prisoner by the rebels, and, later, fought off kidnappers. She asked herself how Lady Theo would manage the situation and got her courage back. "Thank you, sir. That will be all. Wynsham will show you out."

She stood watching, her back straight as a board, until she saw the man enter a waiting hackney cab. Then she raced into the hallway. "Luc!" she yelled at the top of her voice.

He came running. She produced the blue summons and told him what the man had said. He looked serious almost immediately. "We've got to let Lady Theo know. I can't think how, though. I'm not supposed to leave the house."

"Can somebody else go? John Coachman?"

"He doesn't know the area south of the river like I do." Even though he was standing, Sophie saw his body thrum with nervous energy as he thought. "If I leave now," he said eventually, "I'm pretty sure I could reach Châteauguay before nightfall. I'll come back tonight but Lady Theo might have to wait till morning. She's not used to riding rough, like I am."

"But what about me?" Sophie asked, her hands bunching her pinafore. "I'll be by myself. Bert can come right into the house and take me. No one will be here to stop him."

Luc opened his mouth to say something but closed it when Minnie appeared, beeswax and polishing cloth in hand. He winked at Sophie as he put his hand to his head in a theatrical gesture. "Gosh. Golly. I clean forgot, Sophie. Mr. Lofty asked me to help you with that Greek translation of the Peloponnesian War. If we do it now, I'll just have enough time before I have to go off to see Marc."

Sophie followed as he walked towards the library. Just before she entered it, she looked back. Minnie had left the room as well. Apparently, her polishing needed an audience. "You're right," she said, closing the door behind her. "Minnie's watching us. She *must* be a spy."

"She's probably paid by your brothers. Isn't this summons convenient for them? As soon as Lady Theo leaves, you're summoned to court." To Sophie's amazement, he picked a few books up and let them drop to the floor. "There," he said. "That should convince her. Now, come over here so she can't hear. I have a plan."

"What?"

"You were right. There's no one to help you if I leave. Thomas and Eloise are with Lady Theo. I just bet Minnie would find some way to distract Wynsham. By the time John Coachman heard about anything, it would be too late."

Sophie's eyes lit up. "Are you saying I can go with you?"

"No, it's too dangerous. What's more, you'd only slow me down. But, you do have to get out of this house. I'm going to tell everyone we're going sledding. That way no one will think anything about it when you come downstairs looking bundled up. When you go to your bedroom to change, put on three clean sets of everything. Hide your hairbrush and whatever else you need in your pockets. Instead of sledding, I'll take you to Orr's. We'll ask Mr. Christie to look after you. Understand?"

"I can't go to a hotel without a maid. Eloise has gone with Lady Theo. Who should I take? Not Minnie!"

Luc understood the implications behind the question. Young ladies could not go anywhere without a chaperon. "No, you can't take Minnie, that's for sure. We'll ask Mr. Christie to have one of the hotel maids look after you."

"What if he's not there?"

"Then we'll take a room in Lady Theo's name at Rasco's. They know both of you there. You can make up some lie. Like her carriage broke down and she sent you on ahead. I've got plenty of money, so we can pay for everything."

"And I still have most of my pin money," Sophie told him.

"Five minutes, Sophie. Can you be ready in five minutes?"

Sophie hurried up the stairs to her bedroom and began changing clothes as fast as she could. She put her best dress on first, a sky-blue velvet dress that Lady Theo had bought for her to grow into. Then she put her next best dress on, and finally she covered both with an old red dress that had once been her favourite.

As she searched for necessities to stuff into her cloak's pockets, she thought about Luc's plan. Once again, she was astounded by his cleverness when it came to escaping danger. That was one of the best things about him, his knack for making outrageous ideas seem feasible. And this latest idea might work. As long as Minnie didn't find out, no one would think of looking for her at Orr's.

They might, though, if she went to Rasco's. Bert — and probably Bart, by now — knew that she and Lady Theo had stayed there when they had first come to Montreal. Then she shrugged. Luc would just have to come up with another plan.

CHAPTER THIRTEEN

Sophie was fast asleep in her bedroom at Orr's by the time Luc arrived back in Montreal. Only his pounding on the door woke her and Maggie, the maid the hotel had assigned to sleep in her room.

"Sssh," Sophie whispered when she opened the door. "You'll wake everyone."

"Let me in. Do you have any food?"

Maggie tied her dressing gown securely around her waist, knotting the cord several times. After she had lit the lamps and blinked herself awake, she frowned at Luc. "You're not supposed to be in here. Not at this hour."

"I'm her brother," Luc said, grinning disarmingly. "I have to talk to her. It's a family emergency. Can you get me something to eat and some hot chocolate? Please?"

Sophie wasn't sure if it was his smile or the golden guinea that put a sunny expression on the girl's face. Maggie bobbed a curtsy and left, promising to return with a platter, lickety-split.

"Take your time," Luc told her. "I have to tell Miss Sophie about our papa. He's ill, you know."

Sophie barely waited until Maggie was out of earshot before she bombarded Luc with questions. "Did you see Papa? When's Lady Theo coming back?"

Luc took off his mud-splattered overcoat and boots and looked around for some place to put them. Finally, he flung them into a corner, then slowly walked across to the banked fire to warm himself. "It's freezing out there," he muttered, rubbing his hands over the coals.

Sophie pushed a chair close to him. "Sit down. You look exhausted. My questions can wait a few minutes."

"Thanks." Luc sank gratefully into the armchair. After a minute or so, he seemed to get his second wind. "Actually, though, your questions can't wait. Sophie, I didn't find Lady Theo."

Sophie jumped out of her chair. "What do you mean you didn't find her? She wrote the address of the nuns' house on the letter she sent."

"She was there when she wrote it, but since then, they moved your papa back to jail in Napierville. Apparently she went with him. That's all I could find out." When Sophie made a sound of protest, he put his hand up. "There's worse news. About your father. It's bad. The nuns told me quite proudly that a lieutenant-colonel had personally supervised the soldiers who took him. I asked myself, why would somebody as important as a colonel do such an ordinary job. The British must want your papa very much."

"Well, Papa is important. As important as any old lieutenant-colonel, anyway." Sophie blustered as tears flooded her eyes. "Oh, Luc, I was so sure that Lady Theo would sort everything out and bring him back with her. That's why I wasn't too upset when I got her letter. Even when the summons came, I still thought she'd walk into court with Papa and he'd tell Bert off. I never thought they'd put him in jail again." She sat down on the floor beside the fire, pulled her knees to her chin and sobbed quietly.

Luc left the chair and sat beside her. After she hic-cupped her way to a stop, he moved away a little and looked at her. "You're in a right mess, Sophie love. There's no mistake about that. You might as well hear the rest, though. I managed to find one of Marc's cousins. He said he'd try to find Lady Theo in Napierville, but he doesn't even know what she looks like. Even if he finds her, she can't possibly get back in time for court tomorrow."

"What can I do?" Sophie asked, grabbing his hand. "I'd rather go to jail than go back to Malloryville with Bert or Bart."

Luc didn't answer for several long minutes. He simply stared around the room and Sophie wondered what he found so interesting. It wasn't a particularly elegant room, not anywhere near as nice as her one at Rasco's. It was rather crowded, actually, with the maid's truckle bed on the floor taking up most of the spare space. There didn't seem anything funny about it, so she was surprised when Luc suddenly laughed.

"Jail? You'd be prepared to go to jail?"

Sophie nodded.

"Would you care what kind of jail?"

She looked at him as though he was crazy, trying to work out what he meant. She hadn't forgotten the horrible conditions in the Montreal jail he had told her about just the night before. "Well, I'd rather not live on bread and water. I certainly don't want to freeze to death. But you'd buy what I needed, wouldn't you?"

Luc laughed again. A semi-hysterical laugh. "I think I'd bestow my worldly goods upon you."

Sophie frowned. He still wasn't making much sense. Of course, he was exhausted, having been on horseback most of the day. Maybe it was hunger that was making him say such strange things. So it was a relief when there was a soft knock on the door and Maggie entered carrying a platter with mugs and a jug of hot chocolate, some cake, and a stack of sandwiches. Luc devoured the food in short order, then asked Maggie if she'd take the empty plates back to the kitchen.

After she left, he drank his chocolate and turned to Sophie. "Quick. We haven't got much time. Sophie, I have an idea. I've been thinking about it all the way back from Châteauguay. It's going to sound strange, so you have to hear me out. I don't want you interrupting me halfway through."

"I don't interrupt when it's important."

Luc didn't even respond to that. "Sophie, there's only one way to keep you here until your papa's freed."

"I'll do anything," she answered immediately. "Anything."

"Then ... will you marry me?"

Benjamin shivered as he tossed and turned on his narrow cot. The day had brought too many surprises for him to fall easily into a dreamless sleep. Only a few days ago he had wished with all his strength that he would find out who he was and where he was. Now, he knew.

He was Benjamin Mallory of Vermont. He was Benjamin Mallory, a prisoner of the British army, currently occupying cell number 4 in the Napierville jail. They told him he was lucky. He could have had twenty or thirty cell mates. He supposed luck was what you made it.

He turned over on his bed, cursing softly as his arm hit cold stone. He'd figured out, just before it became dark, that his cell could only be about six feet by four. Maybe the guards were right, and he was lucky. He was five foot ten. If he were more than two inches taller, he'd have had to sleep either curled or sitting up. He turned again, desperately trying to find comfort. It seemed especially ironic that he, who had always had so much space, should be reduced to living in such a small cell.

Once again, that vision he'd had earlier of a London mansion flashed into his mind. This time he saw not only the coachman in his blue and gold livery and the white-haired butler, but a bedroom as well.

The bed itself was old-fashioned with its four corner posts stretching towards the ceiling. He knew he had resisted the current London fad of draping curtains around those posts. People said they kept the disease-carrying vapours away. Benjamin, though, had grown up in the wild vastness of Vermont's mountains. He couldn't stand to be enclosed in such a small space.

In his mind's eye, he moved around the room. He remembered the luxuriant sensation of his toes sinking deep into the Axminster carpet beside the bed; the steam from the bowl of hot water on his dressing table, which his valet had brought up from the kitchens; the sound of an oak tree's branch tapping against the window, enticing him to explore the grounds.

If he breathed deeply, he imagined he could still smell the joint of beef being slowly roasted in the old way, by being turned on a spit. He knew he had offered to update the kitchens. Cook had been old-fashioned though, and, after one taste of her roast beef, he had bowed to her superior wisdom. Theo had laughed. She'd told him he was a softie, that women could twist him round their fingers.

He smiled. His Sophie certainly could. He remembered her as an eight-year-old, black-haired imp, scared by nothing. He remembered melting into a puddingly-mush when she turned her blue eyes on him and said, "Please, Papa." He was so proud of her. So ashamed that he'd forgotten her.

As he had everyone else he loved.

Theo. Courageous; staunch in his defence. She'd told him a little about her searches for him, how she and Sophie had settled in Montreal. She'd been far more forthcoming about Luc, the boy she'd adopted.

She hadn't said much about his sons — Albert, Bartholomew, Clarence. He and Jennie, Sophie's mother, used to call them the ABCs. He understood, from what she hadn't said, that the ABCs hadn't bothered looking for him. That seemed strange. Family looked out for family. That's what he'd been taught and what he'd taught his sons. At least, that's what he thought he'd taught them.

He tried to picture them in his mind. Without warning, the vicious headache that he'd hoped never to have again returned. He felt as though someone had struck his temple with an iron bar that had thorns wrapped around it. As he groaned in agony, he felt his body shut down and he knew there were still some parts of his life that his mind refused to remember.

Chapter Fourteen

Luc finished his proposal with a squeak as his voice broke. He blushed, then laughed — an incongruous sound given what he had just asked. Then he looked at Sophie's face and shook his head.

"I'm not joking, Sophie. Don't look like that. It's the only way, don't you see? If I'm your husband, I get to say what you can or cannot do. I can say you have to stay here in Montreal. Even the court would agree to that."

Sophie still looked at him in amazement as she wondered if exhaustion had made him mad. "We can't marry," she told him firmly. "We're children."

"Children who are old enough to marry," Luc replied. "Listen. I'm fourteen and you're twelve, right? That's the legal age for marriage here."

Sophie had once been to a grand wedding at St. George's, in Hanover Square, when she lived in

London. The bride, a niece of Lady Theo's, had married an army captain and Sophie still remembered the wedding's magnificence. There had been seven attendants and three flower girls. The groom's fellow officers had made an arch with their swords that everyone had to walk under when they exited the church. She couldn't imagine such pomp and ceremony being given to a girl her age. Surely, it couldn't be legal.

She turned to Luc. "Girls really get married at twelve?"

"And boys at fourteen," Luc nodded. "Sometimes, anyway. So, how about it? It would solve your problems."

Sophie stared at him, still half convinced his brain was addled. "But don't banns have to be called for three weeks in a row? They're always doing that in church."

"That's for people who have time to wait. We don't. One of Marc's friends got married in a rush because he got something called a 'special licence' from somewhere. It cost a lot of money. Everyone ribbed him about it. That's why I know there's such a thing. I'm not exactly sure how we get one, though. But without your papa or Lady Theo in court, there's nothing to stop your brother taking you back to Vermont. Lady Theo said so herself, remember? Getting married is the only idea I can come up with."

"Luc, marriage is for life. People say 'Till death do us part.' I don't know if I want to be married to you forever. It's not that I don't like you. It's that...." She stared at the banked fire. "In any case, wouldn't I need Papa's permission? Doesn't Papa have to give me away?"

Luc frowned. "I don't know. Maybe with a special licence we don't need him." He looked at Sophie and she could see that he felt hurt by her lack of enthusiasm.

"Luc, don't get me wrong," she told him. "It's a brilliant idea. I just don't know, though. Even if we can get this special licence, does it make it legal? We'd still be married until one of us died, wouldn't we?"

Again Luc frowned. "We'll have to ask Mr. Christie. But if it's the only way to stop your brothers, I say let's do it anyway. Lawyers can always sort it out later."

"Then, what do we do?" Sophie asked, blissfully unaware that she had moved beyond the strangeness of the idea into the possibility of making it work.

"First thing tomorrow, we'll ask Mr. Christie. He'll know. If he doesn't, we'll go to see Marc."

Sophie wasn't convinced that going to jail, instead of to the courthouse, was a good idea. Nor was she convinced about the "forever" aspect of their marriage. She had learned to put little trust in lawyers during the past few weeks. "What about my summons?" she demanded.

"No one knows you're here, except Mr. Christie."

"They'll put me in jail for not going to court tomorrow. It's called contempt."

Luc looked surprised. "How on earth do you know that?"

"I heard Lady Theo explaining it to someone about something else. And I think the man from the court said it as well."

Luc waited while Sophie fussily added a few more coals to the fire. "If you're sure about that," he told her, "we have to ask Mr. Christie if he'll go in your place and ask for a day's grace. That should make things right. He can say that you're sick or something. If it's only a day's delay, surely the judge can be that reasonable."

For once Sophie was the practical one when she asked, "And if he isn't? Reasonable, that is."

"Well, you can't be found in contempt if you had someone there representing you. At least I don't think so. In any case, we'll be married by the next day. We'll both go and I'll say that I forbid you to go to Malloryville. That should work."

Sophie nodded. If Luc said it, that part of his plan should be fine. She still had doubts, though. "If this special licence costs a lot of money, as you say, how can we pay for it? You must not have much left after going to Châteauguay and back."

"I've got enough. Plenty, actually. My father left me a lot. I have trustees in charge of it. They're pretty understanding. As well, Marc was clever. He knew what would happen if things went wrong with the rebellion. Before it started, he transferred most of his money into a trust fund so the government couldn't take it. That's why I've been able to look after him so well. I'm rich. Not in Mr. Ellice and Lady Theo's league, of course, but quite comfortable, as my trustees keep saying."

"You don't act like it," Sophie told him. In her experience, rich boys of Luc's age were insufferable. He, however, was funny and clever. "You're not afraid of getting your hands dirty," she pointed out.

"Neither are you," Luc retorted. "At least, most of the time."

Before their bickering turned into an argument, Maggie returned. Luc quickly said goodnight and left. Only after the door closed behind him and she went back to bed did Sophie realize that she had somehow agreed to marry him.

She awoke the next morning to bright sunshine. Snow had fallen during the night, turning the rooftops into a glittering fairy world. Outside her bedroom window, a cardinal sat in solitary beauty. Sophie watched as he cleaned his red feathers, unsure if he was a good omen or not.

She'd thought long and hard before succumbing to sleep the previous night. Her papa had taught her to try to put things into columns when she had to make difficult decisions. He called them pros and cons. She usually thought of them more simply, as good or bad.

If Luc's plan, the first thing in the good column, worked, she could stay with him and Lady Theo in Montreal. She could keep working to free her papa. She wouldn't have to go back to Malloryville alone. In her mind, she put one tick in the good column.

On the bad side, she wished she understood how they would get out of it. The marriage, that is. She'd never heard of anyone who'd stopped being married — except, of course, when someone died. She knew that much from experience. When her mother died, her papa stopped being a husband and became a widower.

When the cardinal flew off in a blur of red, Sophie realized she'd be doing the same thing. Flying off into a new world. She burrowed deep into her covers as she grappled with the thought. She didn't know if she was ready for anything new. A long time ago, Malloryville had been home. Then, she'd gone with Papa to London and it had become home. In the last few weeks, she had started to call the elegant, four-square granite house that Lady Theo rented in St. Lawrence home. Where would her next one be?

She lay in bed snivelling as she wondered about it, paying no attention to Maggie until she whipped the covers off. "Now, miss," she said briskly. "What's got you so upset?"

"Oh, everything's upside down. It's all going wrong."

"I'd love to have what you call 'wrong,'" Maggie told her in no-nonsense terms as she deftly sponged Sophie's face. She started laying out Sophie's clothes on the bed for the day as she continued. "I come from County Down. Do you know where that is?"

"Ireland."

"Ah, then you know how bad things are there. So bad that me, my mother, my father, and my four brothers all sailed across here to start a new life. My dad kept a-saying we'd live the life of Easy. And do you know what, miss? You talk about things going wrong.... We got cholera on the boat. All seven of us, and I was the only one who didn't go to heaven. I used to wish I had, sometimes."

"What happened to you?"

"The nuns took me in. Me, and I'm not even Catholic. I was young, about seven, so I didn't really understand everything then. I had nothing, though. Still don't have much. Just this job. You do see what I was saying, though. There's lots of people in the world who would give anything to have your wrongs. Now, forget about me. Let's get you dressed. "

Sophie stood and raised her arms when asked to, while she thought about Maggie's story. She knew that, compared to other people, she did live the life of Easy.

She looked at the young maid as she bustled about and asked herself if she could have been so cheerful if she'd had to cope with Maggie's losses. She still had a papa, even though he was in jail somewhere. She had Lady Theo. And, she told herself, she had Luc, who seemed prepared to go to any lengths to help her.

She stopped feeling sorry for herself just as Maggie exclaimed, "Good grief. I clean forgot. Your brother told me he'd be by to take you down to breakfast. Five minutes, he said, and that was ages ago. Better get a move on, miss."

Her words, rather than catapulting Sophie into action, had the reverse effect. Instead of moving, she plumped herself solidly back on the bed. "Maggie? What do you know about marriage?"

Maggie stared at her. "Marriage, miss? The usual, I suppose." She thought for a moment, then shrugged. "It's a long ways away for me, miss. I'm too young to be worrying myself about it."

Sophie allowed her to pull a clean undershirt over her head. "And I'm, apparently, old enough to be worrying myself about it. Oh, I wish Lady Theo were here."

"Well, she isn't," Luc said unexpectedly, having entered the room without knocking.

Sophie and Maggie shrieked in unison, Maggie putting her body in front of Sophie's as a shield against Luc's eyes.

177

"Get out of here," Sophie stormed. "I'm not dressed."

Luc grinned as he winked at her. "You've got to learn to be obedient. When I say five minutes, I mean five minutes. Not half an hour."

Sophie threw her hairbrush at him. "Get out!"

Luc grinned more widely as he backed towards the door. "Three minutes. If I don't see you then, I'm coming back in."

Maggie shut the door behind him with emphasis. "Now, miss. Quickly, now. He means what he says. Which dress do you want to wear?"

"The blue, please. It's the most beautiful one I have." She looked at the friendly maid, considering, for a few seconds. "Maggie, can you keep a secret?"

"I dunno, miss. Depends what it is."

"Nothing wrong, if that's what you're worried about," Sophie answered sharply. Then, she smiled. "Sorry. I didn't mean to snap your head off. It's just ... well, to begin with, Luc isn't my brother."

"I believe I had worked that one out," Maggie replied in a way that showed Sophie her feelings had been hurt.

Sophie smiled at her again. "I am sorry, Maggie. It's just that things are at sixes and sevens in my head. I think I'm doing the right thing. Then, again, maybe I'm not. I just don't know what else to do."

"Yes, miss."

"Oh, Maggie. Forget you're my maid for a moment, will you? I've got to tell someone and you're the only one I can talk to right now. You see, Luc and I are getting married today."

"What?" Maggie stood half-frozen, the curling irons held inches away from Sophie's head. "How, miss? You're younger than I am."

Sophie waited until she had begun to curl her hair and told Maggie a very simplified version of the story. The maid listened avidly, even putting down the curling irons to concentrate better. "So," Sophie finished, "I need you to come with me today. Will you?"

Maggie's raised eyebrows showed her skepticism. "What about your Lady Theo, miss? And, your papa? What will they say to your being married?"

That, of course, was the crucial question. Sophie had no idea of the answer. Neither, it seemed, did Luc when she asked him over breakfast. For the first time since she had known him, he seemed stuck in a thinking rut.

"This is the only way I can keep you safe," he said, over and over again. "I gave Lady Theo my word of honour. It's the only way."

The problem was that Sophie couldn't think of any other way to avoid being dragged back to Vermont, either. Now that Papa was in jail, he wouldn't be able to deal with Bert. Lady Theo was at least a day's travel away. By the time she returned, whenever that was, Sophie might be back in Malloryville.

For once, Sophie was truly on her own. She knew what Luc thought. She, and she alone, would be responsible for taking this step. One so drastic that she could see no way back from it.

Chapter Fifteen

When Lady Theo came back to Montreal at dusk the following evening, her house blazed with light from attic to basement. A strange carriage stood in the driveway, its horses snuffling in the cold, pawing at the cobblestones in their discontent. From the front parlour window, Sophie saw her stop, as though she wanted to question the horses.

She could only imagine Lady Theo's surprise when Cook let her into the house. Not Wynsham, whose job it was, nor Minnie, who should have taken over if he were indisposed. Her concern could be clearly heard in the front parlour when she asked, "What's happened?"

"Oh, your ladyship, we're so glad to see you." Cook replied. "Such goings-on. I plumb don't know what to think. Wynsham and everyone else are in the front parlour."

As Lady Theo strode along the hallway, Sophie wondered if she'd think she'd entered Bedlam. She, herself, sat in one corner of the room, with Luc standing belligerently beside her, daring all comers to approach them. Wynsham hovered protectively close by, holding a silver platter like a weapon in front of him. Sophie's brothers and a constable huddled in another corner, Minnie behind them. Mr. Christie sat in the room's centre, an oasis in the chaos.

Once Lady Theo entered, everyone seemed to freeze. Only Mr. Christie met her eyes when she demanded, "What is the meaning of this?"

When everyone started to answer, Lady Theo held up one hand imperiously. "Enough. Mr. Christie? Would you mind?"

Mr. Christie first helped Lady Theo into one of the chairs before answering her. He waited while Bert and Bart seated themselves gingerly on the sofa. Sophie and Luc moved closer to everyone, choosing armchairs near the fireplace. Wynsham came with them, platter in his hand, and eyed Minnie as though she were a malevolent beast.

While Mr. Christie hesitated and seemed to be working out what to say, Sophie whispered to Luc. "Do you think she's angry?"

"If she's not now, she soon will be," he answered grimly. "Let's hear how Mr. Christie explains everything."

On cue, Mr. Christie turned to Lady Theo. "My lady, I would have hoped to have met you again in better circumstances. I hesitate to offer you refreshments in your own house. However?" He turned to Wynsham as though expecting him to conjure up a platter.

The butler blushed, but remained where he was. When Lady Theo raised an eyebrow enquiringly, he stood his ground. "If your ladyship pleases, I should stay here. You need me. At least until John Coachman arrives."

Bert cleared his throat as though he was going to speak, but Lady Theo held up her hand again. "Mr. Christie! Please. Explain this gathering to me."

The constable, who had remained standing behind Bert and Bart, stepped forward. "I am here with a court order, your ladyship, authorizing me to take custody of Miss Sophie Mallory."

"There's no such person," Luc broke in. "I keep telling you that."

Sophie could see Lady Theo getting angrier by the moment. Splotches of red stained her cheeks, the neckline of her dress looked too tight, and her mouth was compressed into a thin line. "Lady Theo," Sophie began, thinking she might calm things down.

Mr. Christie obviously saw the warning signs as well. "I can see we're wearying you," he said to Lady Theo. "The reason I've been dilatory is that I'm not sure I can explain everything. At least, to your satisfaction. It began, I believe, when you left for Châteauguay. It appears that these gentlemen, if I might call them that ..." he looked across at Bert and Bart, an obvious expression of dislike on his face, "were just waiting for such an occurrence. Your parlour maid, Minnie, was in their employ and she immediately let them know you would be away from Montreal for a couple of days."

Lady Theo stood. She took a couple of angry steps towards her parlour maid. Minnie stood her ground defiantly, and that seemed to enrage Lady Theo even more. "You! Ingrate!" she accused angrily, her eyes spitting fire. "All this time you've been the living ears and eyes in my house for them? You spied upon me in my own dining room, in my parlour? Even my bedroom? You accepted my money, my protection. You ate the food I provided. Out! I want you out of this house, immediately. Right now. Send someone for your bags tomorrow. Just go."

Minnie glared at Lady Theo for a second, then turned to Bart and Bert. "See? I told you how it would be if she found out."

"Out!" Lady Theo thundered. "Have you suddenly become deaf? Get your coat and go. Now!"

She beckoned to the constable. "You're a man of the law. Make sure she leaves my house. Immediately."

Minnie seemed to think about challenging Lady Theo. Instead she tossed her head and flounced from the room with the constable following. Sophie looked apprehensively at Luc. She had never seen Lady Theo so upset and couldn't begin to imagine how she would react to the rest of the news. She looked across the room at her brothers, perched uncomfortably on the old-fashioned sofa. After witnessing Lady Theo's bloodless annihilation of Minnie, they seemed to have lost their eagerness for a fight. Well, almost.

Once the door closed, Mr. Christie cleared his throat and resumed. "As I was saying, the maid alerted her real employers to your absence. They sprang into action and had a summons issued to young Sophie. She had to appear in court the following day for a custody hearing. Young Luc took off on horseback to Châteauguay after you. Before leaving, he briefly explained to me why Sophie couldn't remain here by herself. He asked me to arrange a room for her at Orr's, which I did."

Lady Theo had re-seated herself, but she still appeared to be fuming. "Why?" she asked Luc.

"Because that was the only way I thought she would be safe while I went to tell you what was happening. I know the area and realized I could be there and back faster than anyone else. But Sophie would be alone. You had Thomas and Eloise with you. I didn't think anyone here would protect her." He looked apologetically at Wynsham, still standing guard beside them. "I'm sorry," he said. "I thought Minnie had you under her spell."

Bert shifted his legs as though he wanted to stand and caught both Lady Theo's eye and ire. "Stay right where you are," she ordered. "At least, till I get to the bottom of this. You have some explaining to do, as well. Just remember that. And, now," she said much more gently to Mr. Christie, "resume your story, please."

"The next morning," he told her, obediently, "Luc came to my room very early. We talked for a while. Then he said Sophie was ill and produced the summons that had been served on her. He asked me to go to court to represent her, to ask the judge for a day's grace. This I did."

Lady Theo began with her right index finger tapping against the little finger of her left hand. "Tuesday," she said, pushing the finger back and then touching her ring finger. "Then, the summons was served on Wednesday, and that night Sophie moved to Orr's, right?"

Mr. Christie nodded in agreement.

The ring finger was also pushed back. "So, it's Thursday morning you're talking about? That was the day Sophie was supposed to be in court."

"Right. I went to the courthouse and petitioned the court for a day's grace. His honour, Judge Cameron, wasn't terribly happy but he really had no alternative. He put the case over until this morning."

"And that's when we found out that our little Miss Innocent had been playing games," Bart burst in loudly. "I told Bert he should never have agreed to the postponement. She's a tricky one. Always getting away from us."

"Mr. Christie?" Lady Theo turned away from Bart and gestured for him to resume his story.

Mr. Christie looked uncomfortable and suddenly his collar seemed too tight because he ran a finger around it, trying to loosen it. "Sophie and Luc returned here yesterday, Lady Thornleigh. When she didn't come to court this morning, the judge found her in contempt. He granted Mr. Albert's petition for custody, I'm afraid."

"That's impossible," Lady Theo declared immediately, glaring at Bert.

"It's my fault, Lady Theo," Sophie began, only to be stopped when Lady Theo held up her hand again. She, apparently, had not finished with Bert.

In a deceptively soft voice she asked, "And so, you brought a constable of the police into my house to take your sister to jail? Or, did you imagine you could take her immediately to Vermont?"

Bert straightened in his chair. "I had every right to do so, your ladyship. Young Sophie's become unmanageable. She's disobeyed me, run away from Bart. Now, she's gone too far and defied the court.

That's what the constable was for. To make sure she buckled down under authority."

"You have no authority. That's what I was trying to tell you," Luc said hotly. "Sophie's not defiant. She's not the one trying to kidnap her family. It's you."

When Luc's voice cracked, it only added to his scornful dignity. What he had said, though, caught Lady Theo's attention. "What do you mean, Luc? Why do Sophie's brothers have no authority?"

"He's the one with no authority," Bart interrupted again. "Or respect. You should have seen him, Lady Thornleigh. He took the court order and ripped it in half. It's a wonder the constable didn't haul him right off to jail."

"If there's anyone who should go to jail, it's you. And you know it!" Luc retorted.

Lady Theo closed her eyes and shook her head slightly. "Please, Luc. Just answer my question. What did you mean by no authority?"

"It's simple, Lady Theo. I read the order before I ripped it up. It said that Mr. Albert Mallory had been granted custody of his sister, Miss Sophie Mallory, and that she had to comply with that order or face various penalties. But, as I was trying to tell them, there's no such person as 'Sophie Mallory' anymore."

When all eyes looked at her, Sophie wished someone would interrupt because the moment she'd dreaded had come. The silence stretched unbearably, amplifying the ticking of the Limoges clock on the mantelpiece.

Finally, Bart stood and angrily walked across the room. "All right, you cocky little bastard. Tell us. What, exactly, do you mean?"

Luc stood as well. Slowly he reached into the breast pocket of his jacket and extracted an official-looking document. "There is no 'Sophie Mallory' anymore. Yesterday, Sophie did me the honour of becoming my wife. These are our marriage lines." He turned and looked at Sophie, then extended his hand gracefully. When she stood beside him, he bowed slightly. "Lady Theo, gentlemen. Allow me to present my wife, Mrs. Luc Moriset."

Chapter Sixteen

No one moved or spoke. When Sophie trembled as the silence went on and on, Luc slipped his hand into hers. She couldn't decide if he was fearful, or defiant, or ashamed. If he felt anything like she did, it probably was a mixture of too many emotions to count.

Just when Sophie felt she'd scream, Lady Theo beckoned for the marriage certificate. After reading it, she passed it to Mr. Christie, then burst into laughter. Sophie was startled. She couldn't see anything remotely amusing in the situation.

Wynsham seemed to feel uncomfortable as well. He moved to the sideboard and took a bottle and several glasses from its cupboard. "A small brandy, perhaps, my lady. To tide everyone over until I get the champagne to toast the happy couple."

He served the adults, then left the room. During

the hiatus, Lady Theo seemed to recover her composure as she sipped from her glass. As Sophie watched Bert study her marriage lines, she thought Bart looked panic-stricken. His foot twitched and his fingers beat nervous tattoos on the armrest. "Is it legal?" he asked, over and over again.

"Oh, yes," Lady Theo replied. "As is *this*."

She pulled a sheet of paper from her reticule and gave it to Bert. "Sophie, my dear, it appears you have a plethora of people wanting to look after you. That," she pointed to the paper Bert was reading, "is a notarized statement, signed by your father, that makes me your guardian. In my absence, the court has appointed Albert. Now, we hear, Luc has claimed you for his wife. You have three choices, it seems. Maybe," she said, her voice straying into the sarcastic, "if we remain here for a longer period of time, you'll have more. Mr. Christie, do you have a rabbit up your sleeve? Regarding Sophie, that is?"

Mr. Christie shook his head. "No, my lady. You can rest assured. I won't be among those claiming custody."

Lady Theo took a long, soothing sip from her glass and studied Bert over its rim. "Are you satisfied, Albert?"

Bert allowed Bart to take the documents from his hand and he, too, sipped his brandy. "Satisfied, my lady? No," he said softly. His voice was even quieter when he continued. "However, I accept the fact that both these papers may be legal in this country. I will not accept, though, that either is in the best interest of my sister. Therefore, I implore you. Give Sophie to me. Let me take her home with me and raise her amongst her family. It's the natural order of things. Family looking out for family."

Sophie had already seen Lady Theo show more emotion that afternoon than ever before. Now she became even more terrifying as she transformed herself into an icy, passionless being. "Ah," she said, looking at Bert. "I wondered when the issue of 'family' might arise. I wondered when, for instance, you might ask about your father. I thought you might ask if he was well. Even, where is he? But no. For reasons unknown, you appear to have cut your father from this family you care about so much. And yet, you want his daughter. Why, I wonder?"

Luc ceremoniously seated Sophie again, then stood, his elbows resting on the back of the armchair. "I wonder too," he said. "What's more, I think I know why."

Sophie looked back at him quickly. "Tell me. Why are they always trying to make me go back with them?"

Luc leaned forward and put his hands gently on her shoulders. "Money," he said softly. "You must have a large fortune for them to be this interested in you. And I think we know why they need such a large amount of money."

"Of course," Lady Theo said immediately. "The weapons that the British confiscated. They weren't paid for, were they?"

"Cheating Canadians," Bart stormed. "Said they didn't have to pay because they didn't get them. It wasn't our fault. We took them across the border. We weren't responsible."

Bert looked at Lady Theo. "I am not being an undutiful son, my lady. I do care about my father. It's just that business is precarious right now. The bank is reluctant to extend further credit. It will, however, lend on the basis of Sophie's fortune. It insists, though, on having her physically present in the bank to give consent. It's a mere formality, of course."

"And, if you had her in Vermont, you could make her life a living hell until she agreed. Is that correct?" Lady Theo asked grimly.

"They'd have Elias do their dirty work," Luc told her. "He enjoys that kind of thing."

Bart put a hand up in defence of his son. "He wouldn't do anything to harm her."

As Luc snorted his disbelief, Sophie sat straighter in her chair, unconsciously copying Lady Theo's elegant posture. "Lady Theo. You said I had three choices, right?"

Lady Theo nodded. "Right."

"Then I choose to stay here with you and Luc. We'll get Papa out of jail, then you'll marry him. It will be just like before."

For a short instant, Sophie saw her brothers and Mr. Christie look at Lady Theo in total amazement. Lady

Theo also seemed surprised although she had no right to be, Sophie thought, as she shook her head slightly. She had no time to worry about conundrums at the moment. She turned to Bert and Bart. "Unlike you, I love Papa. If I have money, like you say, then I want to use it to get him out of jail."

"Sophie," Bert said, crossing the room to stand in front of her. "Think about things. Without your guarantee, our families could become destitute. We made two shipments of arms up here. We haven't been paid for either. This could mean the end of the Mallorys."

"And what happens if I don't help Papa? Why aren't you worried about him?"

"He's old," Bart told her, gracelessly. "He's had his day. Besides, he's got all this British money from his fiancée here. No, Papa will be fine. Granddad always said he was like a cat. Mr. Nine Lives, he called him." He stopped when he saw the look on Sophie's face and lowered his voice. "Sophie, think about our family. Think about all of us. This is your chance to help. You don't want to see us thrown into a debtors' prison, do you?"

"You don't care if Papa's in prison."

"It's different, Sophie love. You got to look at it differently. Papa's one person. If you don't help us, the whole family will go down."

Sophie shook her head defiantly. "I don't believe you." She looked across to Lady Theo. "Have you found out why the British are so convinced that Papa did something wrong?"

Lady Theo shook her head. "Only that it's something to do with these confounded guns."

Out of the corner of her eye Sophie saw something like smugness on Bert's face. "What is it? What did you do?"

Bert waggled his finger at her as though she had done something naughty. "Sophie, one last time. Help us. Then, maybe, everyone can win. We might be able to find Clart. And I'll give you my word, right here, in front of Lady Thornleigh and Mr. Christie. Help us, and I'll make sure no one from Vermont comes up here to testify against Papa. If you don't, he'll rot in jail. It will be him or us, and everyone will lose."

CHAPTER SEVENTEEN

After Bert, Bart, and Mr. Christie had left, Lady Theo called Sophie into her sitting room. Luc was left kicking his heels outside the door, on notice that he would be next.

Sophie burst into the room with little trepidation. Her brothers had left the house, presumably for Vermont. Without them to worry about, she could concentrate on the biggest single worry in her life.

"How's Papa?" she asked unceremoniously.

Lady Theo took her time answering. For a fleeting second, Sophie thought her question had taken her unawares. "Sophie, your father has been badly hurt. I believe the nuns who looked after him did not think he would survive his wounds."

"That's what I don't understand, Lady Theo. If he wasn't fighting, how did he get hurt?"

Again, Lady Theo took her time before answering. "A British officer decided he was guilty. He tried to beat a confession out of him."

Sophie stared at Lady Theo, eyes huge in her white face. "But, how could he confess if he didn't do anything?"

"Exactly. That's the very question I asked. But, the army has a copy of the contract for those guns your brothers have to pay for. The signature on it is B. Mallory."

"That means it's Bart. It's certainly not Bert. He signs his full name: Albert George Washington Mallory. It always takes a full line. And Papa writes Benjamin S. Mallory, so it can only be Bart. Did you tell them that?"

Lady Theo's smile briefly wiped the exhaustion off her face. "Yes, dear, I did, but it wasn't much use. The captain in charge of interrogations has made up his mind. He's not going to believe anything I say, because I'm Benjamin's fiancée."

"What does Papa say? Surely, he can convince him."

The anguish on Lady Theo's face was in stark contrast to the feminine beauty of her room. Porcelain shepherdesses graced the mantlepiece, their delicate pinks and blues shimmering in the soft firelight. They looked at peace, almost stupidly so, as though they didn't have a worry in the world.

"What about Papa? I can't believe he'd confess. He didn't, did he?"

Lady Theo reached out her hand reassuringly. "No, child, he didn't. But he has paid a terrible price for his stubbornness. He has a huge scar running down his forehead, through his eye, to halfway down his cheek."

"Does it look terrible?"

"Oh, yes. Benjamin will never be handsome again. But, that scar isn't the worst of his injuries. His head is hurt as well. He doesn't remember things, or people." Lady Theo ignored Sophie's horrified gasps. She seemed determined to get everything out and simply held Sophie's hand more tightly as she went on. "The thing you have to understand is that you have to be very brave. Maybe braver than you've ever been. Because, Sophie, my dear child, it's quite possible your papa won't remember you."

"I don't believe you. Papa would never forget me."

Lady Theo smiled wryly. "Well, I didn't think he'd forget me either. But he did, to a large extent. He remembered meeting me in England and dancing with me. He didn't remember anything more. Not even asking me to marry him, or anything to do with Malloryville."

Sophie looked doubtful. "He can't have forgotten me," she insisted. "He can't have."

"We'll get the chance to know. For once, even the British army agrees with us about something. Everyone wants you to come to Napierville with me and find out."

For a few seconds, the thought of seeing her papa again wiped everything else from Sophie's mind.

"Finally," she exclaimed, throwing her arms around Lady Theo. "When can we go?"

"Tomorrow, if I get enough sleep."

"Tomorrow," Sophie almost shouted in her happiness. Then she remembered the new reality of her life. "What about Luc? Can he come?"

"I wouldn't dream of leaving him behind," Lady Theo said dryly. "And, that reminds me. Sophie, what's it like being a married woman?"

Sophie giggled. "I'm still a girl, Lady Theo. I'm a married girl." She sobered as she saw an expression on Lady Theo's face that she didn't understand. "What is it? Are you angry with us? With me? We couldn't think of anything else to do."

"I realize that," Lady Theo told her. "But, seeing as I'm about to be married myself, I thought you could tell me what married life is like."

Sophie looked puzzled. This was a first for her — tutoring Lady Theo, that is. "It's not much different. Not any different, really. Luc says he gets to decide what I can or cannot do because I had to say I would obey him. I told him that was only when Bert or Bart were around, though."

Lady Theo's smile looked genuine for the first time since she'd arrived back. "Of course. But, Sophie, where did you sleep last night?"

Sophie briefly wondered if Lady Theo's brain might

have been injured somehow, as her papa's had been. She fiddled with the gold locket Luc had given her as a wedding present, and hoped that Lady Theo would see it and admire it. "Here, of course," she answered after a while.

"In your own room?"

"Where else?"

"And, no one else was in your room?"

Sophie hesitated, unsure what to say. "No," she said slowly. Then she remembered something. "Lady Theo, I had the best maid when I stayed at Orr's. Maggie O'Hern. You've been saying I'm almost old enough to have my own maid. There's room, now that Minnie's gone. Could we ask her? Please?"

"I'll see about it when I get back," she promised. "Now, Sophie. Let Luc in. I want him to hear about our plans."

As Luc walked into the room, Sophie wondered if he expected Lady Theo to attack him or something. He'd taken the trouble to spruce up his appearance so that he looked immaculate for once. His jacket had been brushed and there wasn't a scuff mark to be seen on his boots. But he had a belligerent twist to his lips and he immediately stood protectively beside her. She saw Lady Theo bite a smile off her lips as she also seemed to notice this.

"Luc," she said, taking the initiative, "one of the things I've just told Sophie is that her father has lost a large part of his memory. One of his interrogators went far beyond his authority and beat him badly, especially around his head."

Luc looked both disgusted by this news and intrigued. "So that's why they had to hide him."

"They put him into the hands of a woman who knew how to treat him. But, yes. I suppose the main idea was concealment. Being here in Canada has given me an entirely different outlook on the British army, I can assure you. Tomorrow, though, I'd like to take both of you back to Napierville. Sophie needs to see her papa, and everyone wants to find out how bad his memory loss is."

"How bad do you think it is, Lady Theo?"

"I'm not sure." Lady Theo looked steadily at Luc. "There's no doubt that he only remembered me from England, in the beginning. When I left, however, I thought he remembered more than he was telling us. In fact, I'm almost certain of that. He seems to be trying to work things out. Particularly about his sons. I think he's puzzled by what they've done. Or, maybe, by what they haven't done. Like visiting him, for instance."

"And the army has a contract with his name on it," Sophie told Luc. "For the guns. But Papa never signed it. I'm positive."

"And so is Bert," Luc said grimly. "That's what he was hinting about last night. He must have known that one of the contracts would surface. There are enough copies of them floating about."

"You knew this?" Sophie accused.

"I feared it," Luc answered quickly. "It was the only reason for your papa to be arrested. I really think they don't care which Mallory they have. Bert, Bart, Clart, or your father. Sophie, you need to know something. Although they may not have realized it at the time, when your brothers bought those guns and brought them across the border last February, they declared war on England. At least, that's what Marc says the army thinks. It doesn't matter that the guns were never used or confiscated right away. It was war. And the fact that they did it again only makes it worse. They're stupid to come here and risk capture. The army's determined to find them. That's why I knew it had to be about money last night."

Lady Theo nodded. What Luc was saying must have made sense to her. "Then Bert must have nerves of steel to have gone into a courtroom here and used his real name when he tried to get custody of you, Sophie. He's braver than I gave him credit for."

"Desperate, my lady," Luc told her.

"He's horrible," Sophie said, bursting out crying. "He let Papa come here after the rebellion started. He deliberately let him come into a trap. He didn't warn him or tell him not to come. He doesn't love Papa at all, does he?"

There was a long silence while Luc and Lady Theo seemed to have an unspoken debate. Then Luc, obviously taking his duties as a husband seriously, answered. "He thinks of your papa as an enemy, Soph. When Mr. Mallory went to England and took you with him, the rest of your family felt betrayed. Your grandfather was still alive. Marc says the old man was a firebrand. He'd sworn that no part of his family would ever have anything to do with the British."

"And then Benjamin decided to marry me," Lady Theo added.

"That still wasn't it," Luc told them. "I used to listen to them talk with Marc. When they found out that Mr. Mallory was going partners with Mr. Ellice they decided he wasn't a real Mallory. A small part of what Bert said last night was true, Soph. I believe him when he says he would bring you up as a real Mallory, or, what his idea of a *real* Mallory is. He's disgusted because you keep choosing British people and British places ahead of your family."

"I didn't choose you or Lady Theo because you're British," Sophie stormed, distraught because so much of what Luc said made sense. "I chose you because both of you like me. I don't care where I live. Just as long as it's with Papa and the two of you."

Lady Theo smiled at Sophie before becoming practical. "Enough talk. We've a long day ahead of us tomorrow. Sophie, off you go. Start getting things ready to pack. Remember, the maids are short-handed at the moment, so everything you can do to help will be useful. And Luc, a few more moments of your time, please."

Only as she started to close the door did Sophie realize that it seemed funny. As Lady Theo had pointed out, they were a maid short. She had learned by now what to take on short trips. Packing was only an excuse to get her out of the room. Why did Lady Theo want to talk to Luc privately?

Going against every rule she'd been taught, she left the door ajar and tried to eavesdrop. "Luc," she heard Lady Theo begin, "thank you for looking after Sophie so well."

Out in the hallway, Sophie grinned. She could imagine the blush that must be stealing over Luc's face. He hated being thanked for things like that. "You're not angry?" she heard him say hesitantly.

"I was. Initially," Lady Theo replied. "Then, of course, I realized that it means absolute safety for Sophie. Until Benjamin's out of jail, her brothers might be able to persuade a judge that her best place is with them. As a woman, I have no legal rights, you know. Even if I were married to Benjamin."

"Here, in Lower Canada, you do, my lady. Females have more rights here than they do in the entire world. Even France. Or England. My grand-mère votes and I know she couldn't do that anywhere else."

Sophie wanted to find out more. She half hoped Lady Theo would allow herself to explore this side road, but she wasn't really surprised when she heard the conversation shift back on track. "About this marriage of yours, Luc. I've questioned Sophie about it. I realize she has no idea what it means and I thank you for that."

"Well," Luc started, then he must have noticed the open door. "Just a moment, my lady," he said, before closing the door in Sophie's face.

CHAPTER EIGHTEEN

As the coach travelled south the following day, Sophie felt the same desolation as when she had left Beauharnois a few weeks earlier. There could be no doubt that they travelled through rebel territory. The sour smell of burning lingered in the air. The skeletons of barn after barn, house after house, were everywhere. The blackened timbers, stark against pristine snow, reminded every passing traveller of the folly and legacy of rebellion.

Even worse, every now and then they passed groups of country people trudging along the road, most of them with bundles tied to their backs. Lady Theo stopped the coach several times, especially when there were small children, and had John Coachman dispense coins to the more destitute-looking. "It's so sad," she said. "Their husbands are probably in jail. Who knows how they'll survive."

"They're going to America," Luc told her. "Some men have escaped there. Maybe there'll be happy reunions. At least we can hope that they'll be looked after."

Sophie didn't want to think about it. She felt that she couldn't handle much more heartbreak and was relieved when Luc told her to look out of the window. "See that field? You can't see much because of the snow. But that's where one of the battles was fought. One of the early ones. And look, Sophie. There are the church towers. Not long now. Ten minutes, I'd say."

Ten minutes to Napierville, Sophie thought, after finding the twin silver spires in the distance. "Can I see Papa tonight?" she asked for the umpteenth time.

"Probably not, dear. Although, I admit, we've made better time than I thought. Tomorrow morning, though. For sure. Shortly after breakfast. They'll expect us then."

When the coach clattered into the centre of the village, Luc became more animated. "Look, Sophie! See? Over there? That's where Mr. Nelson announced the Republic of Canada. Of course, I was in Beauharnois then, but one of my friends showed me."

Sophie was fascinated by the village. Everywhere she looked, men drove their carioles, a kind of one-person, horse-drawn sled, decorated with little bells. They waved *bon jours* to each other, their *bonhomie* a stark contrast to the burned-out farms in the countryside outside the town. A splotchy mass of grey and dark brown mud, interspersed with patches of snow, separated the higher part of the village from the lower, and Luc happily kept pointing out various landmarks as the coach travelled slowly along the rutted streets. Eventually, it stopped at a red, one-storey house.

"Ah, this is it. Our hotel," Lady Theo exclaimed.

Sophie looked around doubtfully, not understanding how accustomed she'd become to the grandeur of buildings like Rasco's and Orr's. "There doesn't seem room for us, much less Eloise and John Coachman," she remarked.

"We'll fit," Lady Theo told her.

"Hurry up, Soph," Luc told her. "There's still a little light left. I want to show you around."

Later, Sophie would be glad for that period of adjustment to Napierville. At the time, she vaguely knew that Luc was distracting her from thoughts of her papa and was grateful. He paraded her around the village, pointing out various shops and houses, telling little stories about each. To her surprise, half the folk seemed to know him. Châteauguay she would have understood, as Marc had a house there. But Napierville?

As usual, Luc's friends came from all walks of life. Some, from his school, were home for the Christmas holidays. A few were farmers' sons, doing their best to keep their families together, and he invited one back to the hotel for dinner. This was the boy who had come from Châteauguay to find Lady Theo. She felt exhausted by the time Lady Theo suggested bed, but keyed up with anticipation. One more sleep and she'd see Papa.

That night she had lots to talk to God about when she said her prayers — the people walking their way to the United States; the families she'd heard were still hiding in the forests; and, of course, Papa.

Only when she, Luc, and Lady Theo signed the prison's visitors register the next morning did she understand that she'd known nothing about the reality facing her father. A grim corporal read their signatures, his face looking as though he'd eaten broken glass for breakfast. When he muttered, "Another Mallory," Sophie wondered what Luc thought. Should she have signed her name as "Sophie Moriset?" It was so hard to remember that she was married.

After glaring at them for a few minutes more, the corporal finally escorted them to a large office. Colonel Grey walked forward immediately and took both of Lady Theo's hands in his. "You made good time, Theo. Now, introduce me."

"Luc Moriset," she responded as Luc made his bow. "And, this is Sophie."

Not Sophie Moriset, Sophie thought as she curtsied. Lady Theo seemed to have trouble remembering her marriage, as well. She had no time for further thought because Colonel Grey pulled out chairs for her and Lady Theo and waved Luc to another.

They chatted about the long trip down. Then, visibly, Colonel Grey became all business. "Theo," he said in a voice that banished thoughts of disobedience. "I want you to wait here for a few minutes before you come to the interview room. Sister Marie-Josephte suggested that it might help Benjamin if he saw Sophie on her own, without you. She felt seeing her alone might jolt his memory better."

"Isn't he expecting me?" Sophie asked.

"In a week's time. Not today. We wanted to surprise him. To give him that jolt I spoke about."

"Why?"

Colonel Grey's smile was tired. "Because he's my friend and I want him released. Because I'm an officer in the British army and want to find out what he knows. You do realise, don't you, we need his memory back. He has to convince us that the signature on the contract isn't his."

"I can tell you that," Sophie told him. "Papa was in England when those guns were bought. He didn't have anything to do with it."

"We'll see," Colonel Grey told her. "This way."

"Can I come?" Luc asked, looking half prepared to fight the Colonel on this.

Colonel Grey stopped and looked back at Luc. "I think not. I think we'll stay with the original plan. I'll look after her. You wait with Lady Thornleigh." He turned back to Sophie and held out his arm. "Let's go, shall we?"

Sophie was glad of his support when they descended a flight of stairs to a dark cellar. This place is like a dungeon, she thought. She worried about spiders when Colonel Grey led her into a largish room where the only light came from narrow windows set high in the wall. It was too dark to see properly until he lit a bank of candles. Then, she wished he hadn't. Patches of moss covered the bottom part of two of the walls and the room smelt like it hadn't had fresh air since the ceiling was put on it.

In the background, she heard a guard's gruff voice and then the clanking of chains as a prisoner shuffled along the hallway towards them.

Papa!

Then, there was the sound of a hammer and of chains falling onto the stone floor. A minute later, the door opened and her papa limped carefully into the room.

Once he saw Colonel Grey, a wide grin lit his face. "Charles. My friend. It's getting to be a habit. I ..."

He broke off as he glimpsed Sophie sitting on the far side of the Colonel. He looked at her curiously, obviously wondering what she would be doing in the room. Then, he looked startled and Sophie realized that he had worked out whom she had to be. She felt angry, and terribly sad. Deep within herself, she hadn't believed Lady Theo. She couldn't believe Papa would have forgotten who she was. Yet, she had seen the proof in his eyes. It had only been for a few seconds, but it was long enough.

He seemed to understand how disappointed she was because he turned towards her immediately, his arms outstretched. "Sophie! My darling Sophie. Just look at you, all grown up."

At that moment, Sophie didn't really care that he hadn't immediately remembered her. All she knew was that he was in the same room. She jumped from her chair and threw herself into his arms. With the abandon of a three-year-old, she held her arms tightly around him, determined never to let him go again. He whispered sweet, soothing words and she cried for happiness. After a while she cried, as well, for the despair and desolation of the last couple of months. Finally, she cried because she knew that at the end of an hour or so, the chains would be riveted again on to his feet and hands and he'd be led back to his cell. At that point, she feared her heart would really break.

When Colonel Grey asked them to sit, Sophie refused to go back into her chair. She stayed in her papa's lap, trying to smooth his scar while he and the Colonel talked. It wasn't as horrible as she'd feared, but she was glad she'd been warned about it. After a blissful five minutes, there was a knock on the door. Lady Theo and Luc entered the room, and Sophie resumed her young lady persona and seated herself properly by Colonel Grey again.

Lady Theo kissed Papa on the cheek, murmured something Sophie couldn't hear, then added, "And, this is Luc Moriset."

"Ah, Luc," Papa replied. "I owe you so much. More than I can acknowledge in front of my friend, the Colonel, here, I understand."

Luc flushed and looked somewhat warily at Colonel Grey. "It was my honour, sir."

"And his honour and his care of Sophie has landed him into a tricky situation," Lady Theo told Benjamin. "While I was here, there was another attempt to get Sophie back to Vermont. Albert had the courts appoint him her guardian."

"They have no business doing that," Papa replied immediately. "She already has one if anything should happen to me. Send Albert to Mr. Samuel Gerrard of Montreal in the future. He's the Bear's representative in Canada. He'll make sure Bert understands what's what." He stopped, maybe because he saw the expressions on everyone's faces. He seemed half exasperated, as though everyone else had problems with their memories, not him.

"Surely you remember, Theo? Once I realized what was up, I made that last-minute trip to Montpelier. I wanted to make everything legal before I left for Canada. And I did. If anything happens to me, Bear Ellice is Sophie's trustee. You have custody, of course. But Bear's her official guardian. When I signed the partnership documents, I transferred my assets, including Sophie's inheritance, to England. Didn't I tell you?"

Benjamin looked puzzled when he finished. The quietness in the room seemed to drain him, for he suddenly groaned and looked about ready to collapse. He groaned again, then clutched his head in agony. Charles Grey dampened his handkerchief and Lady Theo blotted beads of sweat off Benjamin's forehead. "You should rest, dear. We can come back this afternoon. At three. If Charles permits, of course."

Charles nodded his assent and helped his friend to the doorway. Then, all of them pretended not to hear the sounds of Benjamin being chained up again. Only after the sounds of him moving had died away did Lady Theo turn to Charles.

"Did he remember Sophie?" she demanded. "Is that what sparked this?"

"No. I think he worked it out. Who she was, that is. Wouldn't you say so, Sophie?"

Sophie nodded, her mind churning over the information her father had blurted out. As Lady Theo had said in Montreal, she had guardians and protectors coming out of the woodwork. Having Bear Ellice for her guardian sounded terrifying. He was such an important man. When Colonel Grey's father was Prime Minister of England, he took the Bear's advice time and time again. Mr. Ellice's knowledge of events was legendary. This was partly due to the fact that he had businesses all over the world: in India, the Australian colonies, and the Spice Islands. Much of his overseas investment, though, was concentrated in North America.

Sophie had only met him a few times. He had always been kind, but seemed disinterested in her. She suspected, though, that he'd look after her money as fiercely as Lady Theo looked after her.

"Oh boy," Luc said, breaking into her thoughts. "What your brothers will think about all this."

Lady Theo looked across to Charles Grey. "That outburst was spontaneous, wasn't it? Somehow he reacted naturally. He didn't have to stop and try to think. Does that mean he's remembered everything, Charles?"

"I have no idea, unfortunately. The only thing I'm certain about is that between now and the next time I see him, Benjamin will have a very clever story to explain what he let slip. You may have noticed that he said he realized something was up while he was still in Vermont. That he knew something was going on or about to happen. I'd give a small fortune to know what he meant. Unfortunately, my colleagues would try to beat it out of him again, if I report it. But you could do him a big favour, if you can find out what he meant. It could be the difference between him staying in prison and getting out."

CHAPTER NINETEEN

Charles Grey was right. While Benjamin Mallory's memory might not be in full working order, there was absolutely nothing else wrong with his mind. By three o'clock he had recovered his equilibrium. When Charles questioned him, he claimed he'd forgotten what he'd said earlier, and even though Lady Theo repeated his own words to him, he said he couldn't remember them.

For the first time in her life, Sophie knew her papa was lying. Luc, as usual, said he knew why. "He must have found something out," he told Sophie and Lady Theo later that night. "Think about it. I remember Marc being surprised by that last-minute trip. Everyone was so certain that he'd go with you to Beauharnois."

"He didn't say anything to me. Just that he had some unexpected loose ends to tie up," Lady Theo added. There was an obvious sadness deep in her eyes and Sophie knew that Lady Theo, like herself, felt shut out. Luc, however, seemed excited. He pounded the butt end of his fork on the table while he thought.

"Now, we know Bert really has a money problem," he began in a thinking-out-loud voice. "If Mr. Mallory shifted some of his business into Mr. Ellice's control, that would explain why Bert and Bart are so desperate to raise money that they'd kidnap Sophie. Do you think they know about Mr. Ellice, Lady T?"

In spite of her worry, Sophie smiled. Marriage had done something to Luc. She wasn't quite sure what, though. Shortening names seemed to be one thing. She'd become Soph, and now he was calling Lady Theo "Lady T" with impunity. She wished she knew what they'd talked about that last night in Montreal because, since then, they'd become as thick as ickle-weavers.

As Lady Theo and Luc discussed her papa's surprising news, Sophie decided that Luc was right. As usual. Papa must have found something out. Something about the guns. Maybe Bert had taken money from the mills to buy them while Papa was still in England. Papa would have felt betrayed. It had to be serious for him to sell almost everything in Malloryville and become Bear Ellice's partner. She vaguely remembered Edward Ellice, the Bear's son, talking about selling Mallory timber to the British navy for masts. Maybe that was the new business.

But what had prompted Papa to do something so drastic? Now she realized why Bert must have felt so betrayed when he found that the money was gone. Maybe that was why he seemed prepared to let Papa die or stay in jail indefinitely. In his mind, Papa had become a traitor to the family, just as Luc had said.

Well, she decided, if Papa was a traitor, so was she. She'd meant what she said to Bert. She didn't care where she lived, providing that Papa, Lady Theo, and now Luc, were there as well. She didn't think she could love Montreal as much as she loved the wild mountains of Vermont, but she knew she could try. The main thing, however, was to try to free Papa.

"He's impossible," Colonel Grey told them a few days later. "I can't help him anymore, Theo. He keeps saying he can't remember anything. About the rebellion, or about his sons."

"I know," she replied. "I've wished there were a magical way to kidnap them and bring them here to face him, to force a confrontation. I can't think of any other way to get him to talk. With us, he just closes his lips."

"We can't even figure out what he found out," Sophie added. "We don't know if it was about the guns or something worse. What's more, Bert and Bart seem prepared to let him pay for their sins. Luc says it's because they think Papa is a traitor, but I think they're the traitors."

"Well," Charles Grey said sternly, standing and becoming a colonel in front of them. "Here's exactly what will happen. Unless Benjamin talks, he will be tried for waging war against Her Majesty. There's absolutely nothing I can do to prevent it. I've been shown a few documents that are said to be signed by him. I've told the deputy judge advocates that I, myself, would testify that Benjamin was in England when the first shipment of guns was bought and brought over here last February. They say he could have signed the contract anywhere. Even England."

"But he didn't," Sophie assured him.

He smiled gently. "I know, sprite. But only because I know Benjamin. In my other role, as a hard-hearted officer of Her Majesty, the Queen, I agree with them. The contracts could have been signed in England. On the other hand, they could equally have been signed in Vermont and the "B" on the contract could mean Bert, or Bart, or, Benjamin."

"What other evidence is there, sir? Can you tell us?"

"Ah, as Ben's friend, I can. As a British colonel, I cannot. However, I can say that it stinks. It's very dubious and any good lawyer should be able to shoot it to shreds. And I am going to tell you one more thing that I probably shouldn't. The government is desperate to stop Americans from invading. There have been more raids than I can count from New York and Michigan on

Upper Canada and we hear there's going to be another, from Vermont, sometime soon."

Luc jumped to his feet, knocking over his chair, his face a confusion of surprise and worry. "They know about that?"

Colonel Grey glared at him. "I trust *you* don't know anything about it, young Moriset. Don't forget, don't ever forget; knowledge is dangerous in times like this." He looked across at Lady Theo. "Make sure he learns to forget," he demanded softly. "Or else, teach him to keep a better guard on his tongue. By rights, I should turn him over for interrogating."

Sophie ran across the room to stand in front of Luc. "He really doesn't know anything," she said.

Lady Theo stood as well. "I'll stand guarantee for the boy, Charles. Don't compromise yourself. Trust us, as we trust you."

He looked at Luc once more, then nodded a grudging acceptance of Lady Theo's guarantee. "Fine. But what I was saying is this: the government will do absolutely anything to prevent a third rebellion. That's why some of my men have come to me in tears when they've had to stand back and allow some of the burning and pillaging that's done by the militias. It is not what good soldiers do, though it's what governments allow if they think it will terrify people into obeying the law. But getting back to Benjamin.... I can tell you what will happen in the foreseeable future. There will be more hangings. Not as many as the Loyalists or the newspapers want, and probably more than London thinks is right. Sir John will judge this to a nicety. That being said, he will also be looking for a high-ranking American to punish. Our Ben fits that bill perfectly."

He turned to Luc. "You, of all people, young man, should know how much weight the court martial puts on evidence." He swallowed a little water from the glass on the table, then faced Lady Theo, sorrow in his eyes. "Theo, listen to me. If Benjamin will not talk, and if he is tried, he will be found guilty and sentenced to death. That, I'm afraid, is the brutal truth."

Sophie and Lady Theo gasped in unison. Sophie slumped back in her chair, hearing and believing the note of truth in Charles Grey's voice. Lady Theo wiped away a tear, then smiled wanly as Charles kissed her cheek. "I'm sorry, Theo. For you and Ben. I wish we could find out what he's hiding but, short of torture, there's nothing we can do. Besides, as one of my men said, he's been nearly beaten to death already and he didn't say anything then, so why should he now? The only hope you have is to persuade him to talk."

With that, he left the room, and the last impression Sophie had of him was the sunlight glinting off his gold-embossed sword.

During the next few days they tried, individually and as a group, to get Benjamin to explain how he had come to be arrested. He'd look at them, smile sadly, and shake his head. Nothing changed when Lady Theo repeated what Charles had told her, either. But Sophie noticed one significant thing: her father, who had never been less than loving, asked nothing about Bert, Bart, or Clart after the first day. She knew he was sad about them, but didn't know what she could do to help.

A couple of days after Colonel Grey had left, Lady Theo interrupted their nightly game of cards. They'd leave Napierville the next day, she said. But first, Benjamin wanted to see Luc by himself. Then Sophie by herself. After that, they'd say their goodbyes and return to Montreal.

"Why?" Sophie asked immediately. "We can't just leave him."

"Because he's being transferred to the main jail," Luc told her. He looked over to Lady Theo apprehensively. "I'm right, aren't I? They're sending him to Montreal."

"Luc!" she exploded. "How you manage to get your information, I simply don't know. What I do know, though, is that Benjamin and I have decided that it's best if you return to school. Maybe then you won't have as much free time. You can either go back to the

Royal Grammar School or try the New College or even the British and Canadian School. But you must go to school. Half days at least."

"What about Mr. Lofty?" Sophie asked. She definitely did not want to have to do lessons by herself.

Lady Theo looked as though she had lost all interest in the subject. "Either Mr. Lofty can teach you or we'll find you a governess," she replied.

"What if I go to the B & C? The British and Canadian School?" Luc asked, looking so innocent that Sophie knew he had a plan in mind.

"What do you mean, Luc?" Lady Theo asked so quickly that Sophie knew she had also recognized his look.

"Then Soph could go with me. They take girls," he replied.

"No," Lady Theo said immediately. "Sophie, you've told me yourself how horrible it was in England when the girls there teased you. Just think. Unless your papa changes his mind and talks, he's going to be the centre of a very public trial. As it is, I fear for Luc. I'm scared that he might have to endure all kinds of horrible things said to him because of Marc. I think the worst is over for him, though. Otherwise, I'd keep him home and let him continue to befuddle poor Mr. Lofty. But school's not for you. Not yet. Not until after Benjamin's trial."

On that subject, she refused to budge. They returned to Montreal and, after a few days, a new regimen was established. John Coachman would drive Luc to the Royal Grammar each morning. He'd return at two in the afternoon, collect Luc, and then, after picking up Sophie and Lady Theo, take them to the jail for the afternoon visiting hours.

It was a bittersweet existence. On one level, Sophie felt happier because she saw her papa daily. On the other hand, Papa still claimed that he remembered nothing about the rebellion or the events leading up to it. He insisted that he had never signed any contracts to buy guns, that the signature on the guns contract wasn't his, that he had never plotted with the rebels or helped them.

By the end of February, ten more men had been hanged for participating in the rebellion — five in January and five more on February 15. Lady Theo resolutely made Luc go to school on both those days.

"It's not that I want to see them hanged," he'd pleaded. It's just ... well, what would happen if they changed their minds and it was Marc?"

"They won't, Luc. Rest assured."

A few days after the last five died, Luc rushed into the house. He found Sophie and Lady Theo seated sombrely in the back parlour. "What's the matter with you?" he asked. "Haven't you heard?"

"Heard what, Luc?" Lady Theo replied.

"Have you heard the news?" Sophie asked, almost simultaneously.

"Of course, I have. From one of the boys at school. Sir John told his father last night. Isn't it grand?"

Sophie felt indignant. Sometimes she wondered if Luc understood anything at all. "You think it's grand?"

"*What* are you talking about, Luc?" Lady Theo asked.

"The news. There are going to be no more hangings. Isn't it grand?" he repeated. "Marc's safe; Mr. Mallory's safe."

Sophie just looked at him. "Don't you ever take the time to understand anything?"

"What's the matter with you?" Luc asked. "I thought you'd be happy."

"I might have been. Yesterday. But today we received this." She handed Luc a printed form. "It's a formal notification. Papa will be tried after all. And by court martial, like Marc."

"Oh, Soph. I had no idea. What can I do?"

CHAPTER TWENTY

Spring came to Montreal. The roads, as usual, were in terrible shape. The ice, during winter, had pushed its way beneath the surface, cracking it and leaving some parts of the roads two or three feet higher than others. Other streets were morasses of mud and John Coachman swore almost every time he took the carriage out.

"Godforsaken place," he grumbled. "Had to use shovels and spades for the snow. Now, it's shovels and spades for the muck."

As Lady Theo had predicted months earlier, the government planned to use Benjamin Mallory's court martial as an object lesson. After it, Americans would know they could not invade or fight in rebellions without being punished.

Lady Theo, Sophie, and Luc arrived at the courtroom each morning shortly before ten and easily found seats near the front. People respected their privacy, allowing them to sit by themselves, and Sophie couldn't help reflecting upon the differences between her papa's trial and Marc's.

Everything seemed old hat. No one doubted that he would be found guilty. That seemed a foregone conclusion. Equally certain was his fate. Although he would be sentenced to death, he wouldn't be hanged.

The only people, it seemed, who had doubts belonged to the government. Particularly, the deputy judge advocates. They built their case against Benjamin with slow, painstaking care. But, as Sophie told Lady Theo and Luc, when it came down to it, they only had the single-page contract and one witness: Jean-Baptiste Couture, a boy about Luc's age, whom Sophie didn't know.

"That's what Benjamin thinks, as well," Lady Theo said, then added softly, "He's a fool. He doesn't take it seriously."

"He does," Sophie said hotly, defending her beloved papa.

"Not enough," Lady Theo retorted. "He thinks because he can prove that the signature on the contract isn't his, and that he has never met young Couture, that he'll get off. There's not a chance, as everyone has told him. In fact, even if he tells the truth now, I doubt if anything will change. Oh, Sophie, sometimes I wish your brothers would go to hell for what they're putting your father through."

"He's chosen it, Lady T," Luc put in. "He could have said what he found out about Sophie's brothers long ago. Don't forget that. I think you're right, though. I think Mr. Mallory believes he'll only be fined if he's found guilty. That's why Mr. Gerrard has to be willing to stand guarantee, isn't it? To show that he can come up with the money."

A long time before the first court martial even began, Lady Theo had stopped being amazed by Luc's ability to get information. "Yes," she said quietly. "What's more, I don't think Sophie really expects anything bad to happen. To Benjamin or Marc."

The trial dragged on for nearly a month — weeks longer than the trial immediately before it, which had had eighteen defendants. Like every other defendant, he had to act as his own lawyer. He did a respectable job, arguing every point, even every comma (or so it seemed to Sophie). He even called her as a witness.

Lady Theo made sure she went to court looking her very best. Eloise had curled her hair and dressed her in the blue velvet dress and Sophie felt quite grown up when Lady Theo put a single strand of pearls around her neck. When her name was called, she walked forward confidently. As Luc reminded her, all she had to do was tell the truth. She put her hand on the Bible, when told to, and swore to tell the truth, the whole truth, and nothing but the truth.

After she was sworn in, Papa took over and her confidence fled with his first question, the one that should have been the easiest. When he asked if her name was Sophie Elizabeth Mallory, she felt dumb-struck. Nobody had prepared her for that question. She gripped the edge of the witness box tightly as she tried to think how to answer. If she said "yes," she would tell a lie not only to the court but before God. On the other hand, she wasn't certain if her marriage was legal. Nobody wanted to talk about it and when she tried to bring it up, they changed the subject. Surely though, Papa wouldn't have said "Mallory" if she were really "Moriset."

As she stood in silence, General Clitherow cleared his throat. Sophie looked at him fearfully. Seen up close, though, he didn't seem an ogre and, as time seemed to stand still, she noticed all kinds of irrelevant details about him, like the buttons on his jacket being in groups of three.

He cleared his throat again. "Come now, Miss Mallory, it's not that difficult a question, is it?"

"No, sir."

"Then, let's start over. Are you Sophie Mallory?"

Sophie nodded. Then, before she could think any more about it, she said, "I am."

General Clitherow nodded to Papa, who smiled at her as he resumed. He asked about the last few years: why they went to England; when had they gone; where had they lived; and when had they returned to Malloryville. Finally, he led up to the crucial question.

"Sophie," Papa told her, "be very sure about this. Is it possible that I left England and came back to Vermont last February?"

"No."

Satisfied with her answer, Papa asked the sergeant to show Sophie the gun contract. After she'd looked at it for a few seconds, he asked, "Is that my signature, Sophie?"

"No." She shook her head to emphasize her answer. "No, it's not."

After that, Papa told the court he had no more questions and one of the deputy judge advocates walked across to the witness stand. He didn't seem interested in Papa's whereabouts in England. He only asked what she had liked best about living in London. His voice was gentle as he talked to her and if Sophie hadn't watched any other trials, she would have thought he was really interested in her. She smiled and told him it was the friends she had made in England, then waited for the hard question she was certain he would ask. She thought it would be about Papa's whereabouts the previous February when the first consignment of guns had been brought up from Vermont.

Instead, the deputy judge advocate concentrated on the contract.

"Miss Mallory, you have testified that the signature on this sheet of paper is not your father's. Is that correct?"

"Yes, sir."

His voice became softer and Sophie was glad that Luc and Lady Theo had warned her about this tactic. The softer, the more gentle the voice, they predicted, the more important the question will be. In a voice so gentle that it seemed he was apologizing for intruding, he asked, "Are you able to tell this court whose signature it is?"

Sophie's grip on the witness stand tightened again, until her knuckles became mountains of glacial white. Slowly she raised her head until she looked directly into the lawyer's eyes. "Yes," she answered so clearly that her voice could be heard in the furthermost seat.

"Then, whose signature is it, Miss Mallory?"

"It's my brother's, sir. My brother, Bartholomew Mallory."

There were gasps throughout the court but the deputy judge advocate didn't look surprised. He thanked Sophie for her testimony and dismissed her. "He didn't believe me," she told Lady Theo and Luc angrily once they left the court. "I went through all of that for nothing. I even told a deliberate lie."

"You don't think you were lying when you said it was Bartholomew's signature, do you? Of course, it is," Lady Theo told her.

"No, not that. It's my name. That's why I couldn't say anything at first. I don't know whether I'm Mallory or Moriset. Which am I?"

Lady Theo and Luc looked at each other. Luc gave an almost imperceptible shrug when he looked back to Sophie. "Both, actually. In English circles I suppose you're Moriset. But legally here, women keep their own name. You'll always be Sophie Mallory here."

Sophie thought back to those moments in the witness box when she had agonized about lying on oath and became angry again. "Why didn't someone tell me? I was really scared."

"Forgive us, Sophie," Lady Theo pleaded. "We didn't think about it. When I tried to think about what might trip you up, I never thought of anything as simple as that. Forgive me?"

"You should have," Sophie told her. Her temper cooled after a few seconds. "In any case," she went on, half-apologetically, "it didn't matter. I don't think they cared what I said. They weren't going to believe me."

"They don't believe any defence witness," Luc said cynically. "I wonder what they'll make of poor Couture. He ran away to Vermont after the first rebellion and when he tried to come back, they said he had to testify against Mr. Mallory."

Sophie felt even sorrier for the boy once he was on the witness stand. He first swore that he had seen Benjamin Mallory sign the guns contract in February. However, when Benjamin produced the governor of Vermont's equerry to prove, once again, that he was in London at the time, Jean-Baptiste backtracked. It wasn't February, he admitted. It was September.

"I remember it distinctly," he told the officer-judges as his Adam's apple bobbed up and down and his voice broke into a squeak. "Mr. Mallory came to where we were meeting in Alburg. I watched him read it and sign it."

But unfortunately for Jean-Baptiste, he'd picked a date when Benjamin was in Montpelier, meeting with the governor. Finally, under intense questioning, he broke down and admitted that he was told that, unless he testified against Benjamin, the government would not allow him back into the province to see his mother, who was dying. Everyone felt sorry for him, even when it was obvious he was lying his head off.

Finally, he chose a different date and stuck to it. He had seen Benjamin Mallory, the accused, sign the document in his office in Malloryville. He scratched his head and said he didn't know why he had been so confused.

He should have remembered it was the twenty-fourth of September because that was a friend's birthday. The officer-judges listened to this amended testimony with such straight faces that Sophie wanted to scream. With that, the court adjourned for luncheon.

Sitting in a parlour at Orr's, Sophie looked at Lady Theo and Luc. "It's useless, isn't it? The whole thing. Papa isn't just a scapegoat for my brothers. He's a scapegoat for every American who helped the rebels. It's not going to matter what he says."

Luc looked at Lady Theo. "No. The verdict was decided before the trial even began."

Nobody sat on the edge of their seats when General Clitherow stood to make his final speech to the court. The room was almost empty and his fellow officers seemed to have their minds on their next assignments. When Benjamin stood and heard the death sentence pronounced, Sophie would have sworn that he was surprised. She wondered if his head injury had been more severe than Lady Theo had mentioned.

She, and everyone else she knew, had warned him to expect it, yet he hadn't. He really seemed surprised by the sentence. She wondered if he even remembered their warnings. Lady Theo frowned as if she, too, was puzzled by Benjamin's look of surprise. They had no time for further conjecture. One of the jailers fastened his chains and, after a frantic glance at them, he was led out of the court.

"What's going to happen next?" Sophie asked Luc. But he, unusually, had no answers.

The next four months were difficult. Life revolved around daily visits to the jail. They took Papa and Marc extra food and Sophie spent at least an hour every morning writing letters for the many men who weren't able to read or write.

Sophie enjoyed those times because she felt she was doing something helpful. She sat at a table in the common area of her father's wing in the jail. Sometimes one of the men would be making lunch for everybody from the ingredients she and Luc had carried in. Then, one by one, the men would come in. Some of their letters were to their lawyers; most were to their wives and families. As Sophie didn't write in French, most of the letters were first sent to their parish priest. Then, Sophie imagined, he'd take them to the various families and translate them.

Most of the time, though, she felt she was still in a strange limbo. Nobody visited them and she and Lady Theo were no longer invited to parties or even afternoon tea. Luc's friends reluctantly included her in some of their activities. They had strange ideas about her. She could sit in a canoe, but not paddle. When she tried to tell them she'd grown up paddling and was as good as they were, Luc told her not to bother.

"They won't believe you," he said simply. "Their sisters wouldn't dream of doing anything so unladylike here in the city."

"Aaargh," Sophie responded. "What do they do then?"

"Oh, get themselves pretty. Practise walking about with books on their heads. Find out gossip to tell each other at parties."

"Then, seeing as I can't go to any, what exactly am I supposed to do?"

She talked about it to Lady Theo who, unlike Luc, sympathized. "We can't do anything, Sophie love, until we know what's happening with your papa. But, it might be a good idea to start thinking about where you want to live. If Benjamin's freed on probation, we might have to stay here, of course. I'm still confident though that the government will come to its senses and let him out at the end of the summer. Everyone seems to expect most of the men to be freed then."

Luc's grandmother died in late July and he was heart-broken. Other than Marc, she was his only living relative. Instead of spending time with his friends, he either skulked about the house or visited Marc. One day he came back from the jail with news.

"The court martial got it right when it got it wrong," he began.

Lady Theo laughed and put her hand up in protest. "In English, please."

"Everyone thinks that Marc is going to be transported to Van Diemen's Land, one of the Australian colonies. Somebody said that the ship that's going to take them has already left England."

Sophie focused on one word. "Them? Who's them? Papa?"

"I don't think so. Everyone knows he didn't do anything. It's the men from Beauharnois, probably, and Marc's friends from Châteauguay."

Lady Theo looked thoughtful. "You say that the ship has already left?"

Luc nodded.

"Then I'd better pay a visit to our lawyers. Maybe, they will have heard something. And Charles is in town. I'll ask if he knows anything."

When Sophie and Luc went to the jail the next morning, the place seemed electrified. Men darted from cell to cell, passing on the latest rumour or trying to find out the latest rumour. One man had made a huge chart which he'd put in the common area. It had four columns on it: transportation, probation, exile, and free. Men wrote their names on it.

The chart puzzled Sophie. "What's the difference

between transportation and exile?"

"Far away or close by," Luc answered.

Marc took pity on her. "Transportation means that a person is sent to a different country for a number of years. Most times, it's either for seven years or for life. Exile just means I can't live here. I have to go to the United States or someplace else."

Marc seemed resigned to his fate. He asked Sophie if she could find any books on Van Diemen's Land. And, as if to tempt fate, he'd started a betting pool. Using the chart, men bet on where everyone would end up. The one who made the most accurate predictions would win the pot.

"It seems funny," Sophie commented later that evening when she told Lady Theo about the betting pool. "Somehow everyone is happier, even if they put their own names on the transportation list."

"It gives them a sense of controlling things," Lady Theo told her as she fanned herself vigorously. "It's so hot and still. I'll bet we have a thunderstorm. Any takers?"

Seconds later the sound of thunder reverberated throughout the house. Sophie and Lady Theo looked at each other and laughed. They sobered when they realized it had been someone pounding on the front door.

Wynsham entered the room almost immediately. "An official, my lady. To see Miss Sophie and Master Luc."

"I'll get him," Sophie offered and, before anyone said otherwise, ran to the stairs. "Luc! We need you."

Wynsham waited until Luc rushed downstairs before ushering a sheriff's officer into the room. He stayed by the doorway while the officer handed official-looking blue documents to Sophie and Luc, then escorted him out.

Luc opened his paper first. "It's the official notice," he said. "Marc's going to be transported. But not to Van Diemen's Land," he added, a note of surprise in his voice. "He's going to New South Wales. What does yours say, Sophie?"

CHAPTER TWENTY-ONE

Sophie stared at the blue document, unwilling to break the seal. She knew that whatever it said, a new part of her life would begin. Her hand trembled as it hovered over the seal and she ignored Luc's demands that she hurry up. Only when she saw Lady Theo's tight, set face did she realize how excruciating her delay must be. She pushed her finger in, broke the seal, and read her father's fate in disbelief.

"New South Wales," she said finally. "They're sending him with Marc. Here, Lady Theo. See for yourself."

By this time Luc had reread his notification. "Lady T? Sophie? Look at the departure date. It's two days from now. They've only given us forty-eight hours to prepare for it. How will the people in the country ever make it to Montreal in time?"

As if to punctuate his words, a loud clap of thunder shook the room and Lady Theo came out of a trance she'd seemed to be in. "Fortunately, I know more about New South Wales than I do about Van Diemen's Land. We'll have to shop tomorrow, Sophie, and buy provisions for them. The trip on the boat will take six months or more. We'll have to make sure we send dried food and...." She reached for a pencil to begin making lists. Then, she stopped and looked at Luc and Sophie. "No," she said. "That's the easy thing. The most important thing we can give Benjamin and Marc right now is hope. We have to send them off with the knowledge that we'll keep working to get them pardoned. And they both need to know where we'll be."

"Well here, of course," Luc said impatiently, then frowned. He sat up and the blue notice dropped to the floor. "You're right, Lady Theo. I understand," he went on excitedly. "I could go to New South Wales to be close to Marc. You'd let me, wouldn't you?"

"What about me?" Sophie put in. "You're supposed to be married to me, remember?"

Both Luc and Lady Theo looked chagrined at the reminder. "Let's not squabble," Lady Theo said. "Let's be calm and rational. It seems to me we have three choices. We can stay here where Luc is comfortable, we can go to England, or ..."

"We can all go to New South Wales," Luc finished, his bright eyes showing his excitement.

"I don't want to stay here," Sophie said decidedly. "Neither Lady Theo nor I have any real friends and the winter is horrible. What would we do in England?"

Lady Theo didn't reply for a moment and Sophie wondered if she was remembering her previous home and the beautiful countryside surrounding it. "Well, for one thing," she began, "both of you would go to good schools. Sophie, you have friends at your old school, so I suppose we would live in London. As for you Luc, all of my family go to Eton College. You would go there."

"No, he shouldn't," Sophie said with a bit of a giggle in her voice. "I've met boys from there. They think they're gods. Luc gets into far too much trouble to be a god."

"I could go to school in New South Wales," Luc answered, turning his back on Sophie.

"And I could go to school in London," Sophie told him. She stood and walked across to Lady Theo. "Where could we help Papa the most?" she asked. "London or New South Wales?"

Lady Theo looked troubled. "I thought we had done everything we could," she said. "I was confident that Benjamin would get a pardon. The only thing left to do is petition the queen. That's best done in person."

"Then I think we should tell Papa and Marc that tomorrow. That after they've left, we'll go to London to petition the queen."

"It's a long shot," Luc argued. "Of course, I think we have to make the effort. But," he stopped and Sophie could see visions of New South Wales still dancing in his head. "I think if we don't succeed, we should all go to New South Wales. Marc and Mr. Mallory will need us."

Before Sophie could reply, Wynsham knocked on the door. "Excuse the interruption, my lady. We, that is the staff, have been discussing these developments. Eloise and John Coachman will, of course, go wherever you go. But young Maggie and I would consider ourselves honoured to be considered part of the household. If you go to New South Wales, you'll need a major-domo. I guarantee I will make the travel there as comfortable as possible, and make the house there run even more smoothly than here."

"Thank you, Wynsham," Lady Theo said, obviously touched by his loyalty. Then she laughed. "I think I've just been outvoted. Very well, then. Wynsham, tomorrow you may begin arranging our travel back to England. But keep our eventual destination in mind."

"New South Wales. And adventure," Luc finished.

"New South Wales. And adventure," Sophie repeated, suddenly pleased.

Benjamin stared at the vellum paper in his hand. In many ways, it was what his dear Theo and Sophie had worked for. A pardon. Her Majesty, Queen Victoria, had been graciously pleased to pardon him. He wouldn't have to worry about being dragged off to the gallows anymore. Not even as a scapegoat for the crimes of his fellow Americans.

In the surrounding cells, shouts of celebration mixed with cries of agony as other men read their own sheets of parchment or had them translated. Yes, they had been pardoned. They would not be hanged, but there was a condition to Her Majesty's gracious pleasure.

Within the next few days, most of them in his cell block would be sent to a different jail. One somewhere in her colony of New South Wales. Benjamin thought about it. Since his trial he had seen Charles Grey a couple of times. This outcome was better than Charles had warned him to expect; less than Theo had believed would happen; and far worse than Sophie had prayed for, he knew.

When he heard hurried footsteps in the passageway, he moved to the door of his cell. "Marc! Ça va? What's the news for you?"

"Adventure, my friend. They're sending me to the South Seas. And you?"

"The same. How many will be going with us?"

"About fifty," Marc answered. "Maurice Lepailleur and the Thiberts. In fact, most of the men from

Châteauguay and Beauharnois. Young Levesque's been banished to the United States. That's a shock."

Benjamin smiled. "No, my friend. That's influence."

Marc nodded. Guillaume Levesque was almost as well-connected as Benjamin himself. Marc leaned against the doorway thoughtfully. "If influence worked for Levesque, why didn't it work for you?"

"But it did, Marc. Don't you understand yet? Every single person in my family is alive. My sons have everything they wanted. They control the Malloryville mills and they own half the land around them. Of course, they're not as rich as they planned to be. And for me? I'm well satisfied with the bargains I've made."

"Will we ever know exactly how much you remember?"

Benjamin shook his head. "It's not necessary. Like you, my friend, I see Australia as an adventure. A new start. Theo has already said she'll go wherever they send me. As will Sophie and your Luc. Both of us have families, or parts of them, that love us enough to follow us to the ends of the earth. To the Antipodes, in fact. I'm richer than I've ever been before because of that. You, as well. The only regret I have is the pain I caused Theo and Sophie."

Marc shook his head. "You made them very sad, my friend."

Benjamin bowed his head. "I know," he said finally. "But it was the only way. The only fair way. I was like the father in the Bible. The prodigal son's father. My sons didn't want to wait for their inheritance. Now they have it. Furthermore, the government was right. Some Mallorys had declared war on it. Well, the price is paid now. Clart can leave his hiding place and go home. No one is looking for him anymore. But Bart had better not come to Montreal again."

Marc grimaced. Things were different with his family, Benjamin knew. Marc had trusted Luc, his young half-brother, with his money; he'd obviously trust him with his life.

Benjamin understood. "My family has its traditions, just as yours has. In mine, my grandfather never forgot what he lost when he had to flee Boston with a price on his head. Over the years, that solidified into hatred of everything British, and my boys were brought up by him to believe that hatred excused everything. Even killing. Or betrayal. When I went to London, even though I was representing Vermont, they chose to see me as betraying their grandfather's beliefs. They didn't understand that by doing so, they were betraying everything I taught them. That's the tragedy."

Later that night, he sat on his bed and looked at his cell in amazement. Almost every last inch of it was jammed with boxes, and he imagined Marc's room looked the same. Theo had gone on a massive buying spree once she had heard their news. Someone must have told her it would take six months to reach Sydney. Every possible thing needed for a long voyage and life in a hot climate had been purchased. Or, at least, as much as could be bought in Montreal.

He had tins and tins of tooth-cleaning powder. About a dozen boxes of tobacco. He imagined she thought he could use them as trading-goods, seeing that he didn't smoke. There were yards of mosquito netting, ointments, sets of light, cotton clothing. There were books to while away the time on the long voyage. Umpteen packs of cards.

He sat against the stone wall and closed his eyes. Overall, he was grateful for his memory loss, particularly since no one knew exactly what he did or did not remember. He hadn't had to lie in court. Not much, anyway. As well, he thanked God that his life had been spared. Charles had been certain that Bart and Clart would have been hanged if they had been caught, even if their trial had been the last one.

Lastly, he picked up his Bible. It fell open at the page in John's gospel that he had used for solace so frequently during the past few months: "Greater love has no one than this — that he lays down his life for his friends."

He no longer called his sons his friends. He, more than anyone, knew they had defrauded him and allowed him to assume blame for their misdeeds. Once his trial had begun, they could have come forward to save him, but they hadn't. They hadn't written him or sent messages of concern. He guessed they would never feel clean again.

Even with half a mind though, he had thwarted them. His beloved Sophie and her inheritance were safe. His incomparable Theo had stood by him, fighting courageously. When he thought about it all, he had so much to be grateful for. He, Theo, Sophie, and young Luc would make their own fortunes and adventures in Sydney, New South Wales.

He laughed as he considered one last thing. Was Sophie's marriage, such as it was, legal there?

HISTORICAL NOTE

Sophie and Luc are completely fictional. Sophie's father, however, is very loosely based on an American from Vermont. Benjamin Mott was tried for treason and levying war. He seems to have wandered into Canada at a particularly inopportune time and watched one of the battles from the basement of a church. Luc's brother is based on Jean-Marie-Léon Ducharme, and the details about Marc's trial reflect this.

The courts martial of 1838 are the best-documented trials in nineteenth century Canadian legal history. Transcripts of eleven of the fourteen trials were published in 1839 (*Report of the State Trials held before a Court Martial...*). Even though the magistrate, John McDonald, lied under oath on the stand, Ducharme was convicted of treason and sent to Australia. It is uncertain whether or not Benjamin Mott was involved in supplying guns for the rebellion. The prosecution certainly didn't prove its case. Nevertheless, Mott sailed for New South Wales together with Ducharme and fifty-six other men at the end of September 1839. As stated in *Sophie's Treason*, the courts martial of 1838–39 had little to do with justice or the law. They were political trials, designed to intimidate the French-Canadian people and to prevent them rebelling a third time. Innocent people were convicted, evidence was ignored or manipulated, and the punishments depended upon who the rebels were and where they lived rather than their degree of involvement in the rebellion.

Those who wish to study the situation further can read my analysis of the court martial in *A Deep Sense of Wrong*, published by The Dundurn Group in 1995 and by Allen & Unwin in 1996.

Much too frequently when we study history we read about injustices and wrongs. Most of its heroes are larger than life. The unassuming, good people rarely are mentioned. Colonel Grey, however, seems the exception. From everything I've read, Charles Grey was as nice a person and as conscientious as he appears in this story. He tried to limit the vicious punishments inflicted by the militia and regretted his inability to do more. In so many ways, he was a nice guy who didn't finish last.

Beverley Boissery
November 2006

Acknowledgements

Many thanks for the following for their criticisms and support:

> Melanie Anastasiou
> Chris Greenwood
> Kirk Howard
> Paul O'Rourke
> Elizabeth Pieters
> Susan Pieters
> Lorna Phillips
> Bronwyn Short
> Kathy Tyers
> Cathy Wilson

I am deeply appreciative of Barry Jowett's advice and editing; Kathy Tyers' fine-tooth comb in respect of point of view wanderings; and Chris Greenwood's maintenance of the family tradition. He's proofread almost everything I've written.